Russell moved first

At least Meg thought he did. He stepped toward her, forcing her to tilt her face to maintain eye contact. In some vague, barely functioning corner of her mind she saw him lift a hand. Felt the warmth slide against her face.

This was Russell. She'd built so many dreams on him. Had pinned so many hopes on him. And for a while they'd been so good together. That's what she remembered now. Those good times…

She was moving then, toward him, pushing up on her toes with a longing that seeped through her like water from a ground spring.

"Meggie," he murmured, and then she wasn't thinking anymore. Was only feeling. And remembering.

Wanting.

Dear Reader,

Like most girls, I grew up dreaming of my wedding day: my dress, the music, my bridesmaids...and of course, the man I would marry. But my dreams pretty much stopped with that big day, as if it were the end rather than the beginning. Sure, I dreamed of becoming a mother, but it was an abstract idea.

What I've learned—as a veteran of a two-decade union!—is that marriage takes work. All that wonderful passion from the beginning eventually settles into routines. Life happens. People grow. Dreams don't always come true. And that's where the real challenges begin. That's where love meets its ultimate test.

What happens, I sometimes wonder, when two people lose each other along the way? Lose themselves? Can love survive? Can you get it back?

Out of these questions came Russell and Meg Montgomery, a couple on the brink of saying goodbye forever when life throws them a major curveball. Now, with the future of a young child in the balance, they must discover if the life they once dreamed of is still within their reach...this time for keeps.

I love to hear from readers! Please contact me through my Web site at www.JennaMills.com.

Happy reading,

Jenna Mills

This Time for Keeps
Jenna Mills

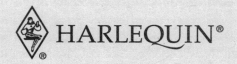

TORONTO • NEW YORK • LONDON
AMSTERDAM • PARIS • SYDNEY • HAMBURG
STOCKHOLM • ATHENS • TOKYO • MILAN • MADRID
PRAGUE • WARSAW • BUDAPEST • AUCKLAND

If you purchased this book without a cover you should be aware
that this book is stolen property. It was reported as "unsold and
destroyed" to the publisher, and neither the author nor the
publisher has received any payment for this "stripped book."

Recycling programs
for this product may
not exist in your area.

ISBN-13: 978-0-373-71659-3

THIS TIME FOR KEEPS

Copyright © 2010 by Jennifer Miller.

All rights reserved. Except for use in any review, the reproduction or
utilization of this work in whole or in part in any form by any electronic,
mechanical or other means, now known or hereafter invented, including
xerography, photocopying and recording, or in any information storage
or retrieval system, is forbidden without the written permission of the
publisher, Harlequin Enterprises Limited, 225 Duncan Mill Road,
Don Mills, Ontario, Canada M3B 3K9.

This is a work of fiction. Names, characters, places and incidents are
either the product of the author's imagination or are used fictitiously,
and any resemblance to actual persons, living or dead, business
establishments, events or locales is entirely coincidental.

This edition published by arrangement with Harlequin Books S.A.

For questions and comments about the quality of this book
please contact us at Customer_eCare@Harlequin.ca.

® and TM are trademarks of the publisher. Trademarks indicated with
® are registered in the United States Patent and Trademark Office, the
Canadian Trade Marks Office and in other countries.

www.eHarlequin.com

Printed in U.S.A.

ABOUT THE AUTHOR

Jenna Mills doesn't remember a time when she wasn't playing matchmaker. From Barbie and Ken to the Professor and Mary Ann, Jenna always wanted love to prevail. It was only natural that she turned this obsession into a career—and her own happily-ever-after. A Louisiana native living in Texas, Jenna lives with her husband of two decades and their two young children.

Books by Jenna Mills

SILHOUETTE ROMANTIC SUSPENSE

1461—THE PERFECT STRANGER*
1468—A LITTLE BIT GUILTY*
1482—SINS OF THE STORM*

*Midnight Secrets

Don't miss any of our special offers. Write to us at the following address for information on our newest releases.

Harlequin Reader Service
U.S.: 3010 Walden Ave., P.O. Box 1325, Buffalo, NY 14269
Canadian: P.O. Box 609, Fort Erie, Ont. L2A 5X3

Every book has its own tone and texture, and its own path to creation. This book would not be without two majorly wonderful people: my husband, Chuck, for all the raw material; and my awesome editor, Wanda, for the chance… and the wise counsel.

You're both incredible!

PROLOGUE

EVEN IN SLEEP, SHE KNEW he was gone.

Megan Montgomery opened her eyes against the hazy light of early morning and reached beside her. The soft cotton sheet and down comforter, both a rich tartan plaid of navies and reds, lay flat. The feather pillow was fluffed. There were no wrinkles, no indentations, no warm places. Absolutely no evidence of the destruction Russell Montgomery could wreak on a bed.

After all this time, the chill on her skin made no sense. *Especially now.*

With a drowsy stretch, Meg drew a hand to her stomach, where beneath the cool silk of her nightgown the swell made her heart sing. Four years in the making; four months until her arrival. Or his.

After today, she would know.

They would know.

On cue, the little one fluttered, and Meg smiled. As much as she wanted to savor the moment, even more she wanted to share it. With a quick glance at the clock, she slipped out of bed and padded from the big bedroom.

Music drifted through the century-old, but newly renovated, house. Soft, lilting strains drew her down the hallway, to the small, east-facing room that had sat empty for years.

The soft, buttery-yellow glow stopped her. He worked quietly, deliberately—just as he did everything.

His chest and feet were bare, his jeans faded and low-slung. Together, man and paintbrush moved in symbiotic rhythm, the muscles of his bare arms and shoulders bunching and releasing with each smooth, even stroke.

The night before, the room had been boring builder-beige. Now the nursery-to-be beckoned like morning sunshine. That had been their intent.

The symbolism appealed.

"Looks good," she murmured, her voice still thick from sleep.

Russell turned, and despite the familiarity between them, her breath caught. His dark copper hair was mussed, his strong jaw in need of a razor. And his smile...it was slow, languorous. "You caught me."

The words were playful, but she knew her husband well enough to see the fatigue in the dark green of his eyes, the sharp glint of something he clearly did not want her to see. Three walls were painted, including trim. Even working at a brisk pace, he couldn't have slept for more than an hour or two.

He'd been acting oddly ever since the phone call that had jarred them from sleep a few days before. He'd left the bed, talked in hushed tones. Told her there was nothing to worry about.

She was trying to believe him.

"Didn't mean to wake you," he said, changing the subject the way he always did when he sensed she was about to prod too close to something he wasn't ready to share. He put down the brushes, crossed to her.

"You didn't." She took his hand and drew it to her belly. "Your son did."

Almost instantly, a twinkle came into Russ's eyes. "You mean my daughter."

Pushing up on her toes, Meg brushed her lips across his. "Maybe," she murmured indulgently, loving the soft scrape of his whiskers. Most men were obsessed with having sons, but all Russell talked about was having a little girl.

"With eyes of blue like her mum's," he said, lapsing into the brogue of his childhood. They'd known each other for six years, been married four. The echo of a Scottish accent shouldn't still inspire that quick little rush. But it did. It was such a disconnect coming from a man who always looked ready to tackle the great outdoors.

"Blond hair," he added while his fingers wove through hers.

Somehow, his touch was as gentle as his words.

"A sweet little smile—"

"Careful what you wish for, Montgomery," she teased, grinning up at him. "You really think you can handle two of us?"

The corners of his eyes crinkled. "Watch me."

She planned on it.

"Wee one must have gone back to sleep," he said, but Meg wouldn't let him take his hand from her stomach. She loved the warmth of his palm against her chemise, loved looking down to see his fingers splayed against her belly.

"Just wait," she whispered.

His frown caught her by surprise. "Can't," he said. "I've got a breakfast meeting over at the Manor."

She stepped back. "Everything okay?"

"Just somebody I used to work with."

"From New York?"

"London," he said, returning to pour the remaining yellow paint back into the can.

Questions surged like the floodwaters that had almost inundated their home the month before, but like a make-shift dam, Meg held them back. They'd been through this before. He'd made his choice, made a clean break, walked away. He didn't miss his old life, didn't want to go back.

Still, curiosity needled through her. As publisher and editor-in-chief of the *Piney Woods Gazette,* that was her job, after all. To ask questions.

It's how they'd met.

"Anyone I know?"

"No."

The vagueness of his answers was not lost on her. Clearly he didn't want to talk about this old colleague—or what they would be discussing. But she knew. A photojournalist, Russ had been at the top of his field when he'd turned his back on it all—the acclaim, the travel. The freedom.

For her.

Someone was always trying to lure him back. "Well, give her my—"

"Meggie." He was across the room in a heartbeat, leaning down to take her face in his hands. "Sean. His name is Sean. We—"

"Russ—"

"—did a few ride-alongs together in Iraq. He's with the BBC—"

"You don't have to—"

"I'm here." The ferocity in his voice made her heart slam. "With you, Meggie. It's where I want to be."

She swallowed hard. She knew that. She did. And if she ever had any doubt, she had only to look at the gallery of framed photographs lining the hallway. From their honeymoon in the Scottish Highlands to an afternoon picnic among the Texas bluebonnets, the moments were all there, captured. *Preserved.*

The surge of raw emotion was new to her. Hormones, she figured. Her girlfriends told her it was perfectly normal, but she'd cried more since becoming pregnant than she had in the past few years, combined.

Her cousin Julia promised this was just the beginning.

"I know," she whispered.

Russ slid his hand back down to cup the newly formed bump. "And at eleven o'clock I'll be with you at Dr. Brennan's."

Meg smiled. At the last sonogram, their little one had waved, then gone right back to sleep. "Promise?"

"Promise," he said with a long, hard kiss. "I'll be there."

CHAPTER ONE

Two and a half years later

WHISPERS OF MORNING SUN leaked through the blinds, casting the small room in an ethereal glow. A cloth doll sat in the rocking chair. A soft pink towel lay on the changing table. And in the far corner, the crib stood in shadow. That was by design. Meg wasn't sure what she'd been thinking, putting a baby in the room that was first to greet the morning. Actually she was pretty sure she hadn't been thinking at all.

Pure emotion, much like pure adrenaline, had a way of sending logic straight out the window.

She slipped closer, careful not to step on the blocks or squeaky teething toys scattered across the rug. Just the slightest sound, and her morning routine would shatter before she even made it to the shower.

Little Charlotte slept. She lay sprawled on her back, her arms thrown over her head, her soft yellow blankie long since discarded. No matter how many times Meg crept in to cover the baby, Charlotte persevered. In those first few fragile weeks, Meg had even slept on the floor.

The swell of pure, unchained emotion still caught her by surprise. This was her favorite time of day, when it was still and quiet, before the craziness began. Little Char looked so peaceful. Her chubby cheeks were relaxed, her sweet little mouth slightly parted. And the baby-fine hair, as red now as the day she was born. She looked so like—

Meg blocked the thought, didn't want the memory. She had a day to start and not a second to spare. Resisting the temptation to retrieve the blanket yet again, she slipped back into the hallway, all too aware of the light steadily encroaching upon the moss-green wall.

One of these days, she'd find time to paint.

In the bathroom, the blast of warm water from the shower felt good. She lingered, indulged in a new lavender body wash her cousin had insisted she try. By the time she turned the water off, she was a good ten minutes behind schedule—and Charlotte was crying.

Grabbing a towel, Meg dried off as she ran from the bathroom down the hardwood of the hallway. Charlotte's screams grew louder, coming in virtual stereo between the now brightly lit nursery and the baby monitor. By the time Meg raced into the room, Charlotte had her chubby little hands wrapped around the crib rail and was working hard to hike her leg over the edge.

"Oh, sweetie," Meg muttered, securing the towel around her as she hurried across the room. The vivid green of Charlotte's eyes swam with frustration—tears made her face splotchy.

"Mama-mama-mama." She sniffed between wails, lifting her little arms toward Meg.

"I'm here," she cooed, and somewhere deep inside, an echo stirred. "I'm here, baby." *With you.* Swooping her from the crib, Meg drew Charlotte close. "I've got you now."

And I'm never going away.

Charlotte burrowed closer, sweet fists closing tight around the flesh of Meg's arms. "Mama-mama…" With

14 THIS TIME FOR KEEPS

the babbling, she nuzzled toward Meg's chest. "Baba-baba…"

Meg's throat tightened. "Bottle," she murmured, grabbing at the towel that kept sliding toward her waist. "You've been such a good girl," she said, heading for the kitchen. "Staying in your bed all night."

About half the time, she ended up cuddled next to Meg.

"You must be hungry," she continued in a soft, sing-song voice. "Let's get you some formula."

Charlotte pulled back and gazed at Meg with a longing that threatened to break her heart all over again.

It wasn't so long ago that Meg had been quite sure there was nothing left to break.

"I know, sweet girl," she whispered. "I know. I miss her, too." Closing her eyes, she let the memories form, the tears and laughter, the smiles…the promises.

There'd been a lot of those.

"Let's get you that bottle," she said, easing Charlotte to the floor. Sweeping had become part of her nightly routine. "Here are your pots," she added, scooting the nesting toy closer. "We'll cook together."

The eleven-month-old plopped down in front of the dishwasher, her tight little pajamas reminding Meg of a pink floral baby sausage. In fire-resistant fabric—the considerations of parenthood were a whole new world.

But it was a world she'd desperately wanted.

As the baby banged the plastic pots together, Meg turned on the water and got the coffee going, measured out formula and poured Cheerios for both of them.

She was opening the fridge when her cell phone rang. Twisting back toward the table, she grabbed the phone and flipped it open. "I'm up, I'm up," she said by way of greeting.

Julia's calls had become an everyday ritual.

"Good," her cousin, the self-appointed alarm clock, said. "That's a start."

Cradling the phone between her ear and shoulder, Meg reached for the milk—and lost her towel. "Oh, crap."

Julia laughed. "You were saying?"

"I—" Forgot. Somehow in her rush to soothe and feed Charlotte, she'd completely forgotten that she'd yet to get dressed. "My hair is wet."

"Usually happens when you take a shower," Julia said. "The key is to dry it before you come to work."

Lately, that didn't always happen.

"Or wash it at night," her cousin went on as Meg rifled through a basket of laundry for clean underwear. "That's what I started doing after Austin." Mother of an almost teenager, Julia ran her family like a drill sergeant. If there was a problem, Julia had a solution. She could hold down a job at the paper, she could cook, she could clean, she could keep her son in line, and still have time for a pedicure.

Meg hadn't quite gotten there yet.

"I know, I know." She struggled into her panties and fastened her bra. "It's just…" There'd been so many changes in such a short period of time. And nowhere near enough sleep. "I'll try."

Julia didn't miss a beat. "And you'll do great. But until then, I'm guessing you need me to cover for you."

Meg blinked. Cover for her?

"The meeting?" Julia went on, reading Meg's mind, as always. Only four days separated them in age. Most of their friends referred to them as twins born to different mothers. It was only natural that they worked together at the *Gazette*. "You know...breakfast? Henry? Veronica?"

Meg's lawyer—and her accountant. Of course. To discuss the *Gazette*'s finances—and how long they could continue operating at a loss. Meg herself had scheduled the meeting. Breakfast had been the only time available. The rest of the day was consumed by an editorial meeting then an all-afternoon planning meeting for the Wildflower Festival. It was less than a week away and the silent auction benefiting the March of Dimes was still up in the air. Plus she and Charlotte had a photo shoot scheduled.

"I'll be there," she said, tearing at the dry cleaning draped over a chair. The office was only a few miles away. "Give me twenty—"

"Meg."

She shoved the tangled mess of wet hair back from her face. All she needed was a comb—

"Stop it."

She stilled, her hands fisted against the linen of her favorite black blouse, not because of her cousin's words. But because of the gentleness in her voice. The quiet understanding.

"Don't," she whispered.

"It's going to be okay," Julia said quietly. "I promise."

Meg squeezed her eyes shut.

"You can *do* this."

She swallowed. "I know."

"We're here for you...all of us. You're not alone."

The smile was automatic. She had the greatest friends

in the world. "I know," she said again, and this time her voice was a little stronger.

"I just…" Julia let out a rough breath. "I don't understand. Did his parents call again?"

Briskly, Meg stepped into her favorite cargo pants. "Yesterday."

"Did you call them back—"

"No."

"Meg, you can't—"

"No," she said again, this time firmer. She'd only spoken to Russell's family once in almost two years. She had neither the time nor the interest to cater to them now. They'd had more than enough chances. "There's no reason to."

"There's every reason to. You can't ignore them and hope they'll go away. She's their granddaughter. They have a right—"

The thud of wood against wood, followed by shrieking, stole the rest of Julia's words. Meg swung toward the kitchen—no longer saw the baby.

"I have to go!" She dropped the phone and ran toward the wails, found Charlotte on the floor of the dining room—underneath one of the big antique chairs.

"Char!" Meg was by the baby's side in a heartbeat, on her knees and yanking the heavy chair away, scooping Charlotte into her arms. "Are you okay—" The nasty red welt on the side of her forehead told Meg what she needed to know.

She'd forgotten. In her rush to get breakfast and get dressed for the meeting she'd spaced, she'd forgotten about Charlotte. She'd set her down on the floor to play, completely overlooking the fact that Charlotte could now pull up and cruise.

"I'm so sorry," she murmured, gently inspecting the

emerging goose egg. "So sorry," she said again, and this time the dam broke, and the tears came. Wearing only her bra and panties, her hair still damp, she cradled the baby in her arms and buried her face against Charlotte, pressing soft kiss after soft kiss against bright red hair. "I'm trying," she promised. *"I'm trying."*

But she'd never planned to do this alone.

Like a sweet little angel, Charlotte nuzzled closer, once again lifting her mouth to root at Meg's breast. "Mama-mama…"

The tears came harder. "I know." She gulped. "I know." And she did. She could love this child of her heart and care for her, feed her and rock her and cradle her, give her every second of every day, every drop of time and energy she had, every creature comfort imaginable.

But she could never give her niece the one thing she wanted—*needed*—the most.

Her mother.

THE BIG GREEN BANNER stretched high over Main Street, secured to light posts on either side of the road.

Join Us For The Flowers…Stay For The Fun!

Meg tensed as she zipped beneath, barely cruising into the intersection before the light turned red. The festival had become an annual rite of spring in Pecan Creek, attracting visitors from all across Texas and Louisiana. This year she'd proposed extending their marketing to include Oklahoma and Arkansas. East Texas wasn't that far a drive from either, and if they could attract a hundred or so new attendees, the extra dollars would go a long way toward helping local merchants.

In the historic district, restaurants and hotels saw a significant jump in business. The gift shops ran special promotions. The high school band used money from the bake sale to fund their annual day trip to Six Flags in Arlington. The moms' club counted on the sales from their cookbook to fund the local women's shelter.

Meg wasn't sure what had possessed her to take on the extra responsibility. Of course, when she'd stepped forward, she'd had little else to fill her days. Or her nights. The *Gazette* had not yet started to hemorrhage money—and her sister-in-law, Ainsley, had been beautifully, gloriously alive. Vibrant. *Pregnant.* They'd been over-the-moon excited.

The memory hurt.

Zooming past the row of shops and restaurants eagerly awaiting the onslaught of tourists, Meg headed for the small parking lot on the corner. Across the street sat the renovated former general store that now served as the main office for the *Piney Woods Gazette.* The paper had been in Meg's family since her great-grandfather had founded it over a hundred years before.

She was not going to let it fold on her watch.

Throwing the car in Park, Meg grabbed her briefcase and all but ran to the office.

Henry and Veronica were long since gone.

"They left some financials for you to review," Julia explained as soon as Meg walked inside. She took the thick folder and glanced down, cringed at the title greeting her: Mid-America Media Acquisition Offer.

"Henry was going to talk to some of the other papers—"

"He did," Julia said, walking with Meg step for step. While Meg had forgone her linen suit in favor of the camo cargos and black T-shirt she preferred, her cousin looked dressed for a job interview in New York. Pecan Creek was a small, sleepy town. Casual. Everyone didn't

quite know everyone, but someone always knew someone, who knew someone. Three degrees of separation,
they joked.

There was no need for a severely tailored navy
suit.

But Julia was…well…Julia.

Meg had never understood why her cousin stayed.

"It's all in there," Julia said. "He talked to the editorial staff at three different regionals. His notes are in
the back."

Meg flipped through the folder, saw the pages in
question. "Great." But her stomach knotted. It was
a good offer, the kind of money that could keep the
Gazette—and all of its employees—afloat. But it also
meant the end of a legacy forged a century before.

Meg tossed the folder on a desk badly in need of
straightening, then dropped her briefcase in the chair
and headed toward the break room. "Just give me a few
minutes to get some coffee and we can get started with
the staff meeting."

"Got it," Julia said. "I can't wait to tell you what I
found out about the Brookhaven Institute. I'll bet my
last dollar there's more than sleep research going on
there."

Meg tossed her cousin a look, but before she could
say anything about Julia's wild conspiracy theories, their
office manager joined them. After all this time, it still
felt weird thinking of Lori Bradshaw as an employee.
Meg could still see her on the first day of school freshman year, a shy, slightly pudgy girl with braces, glasses
and the most ridiculous pigtails imaginable.

"How's that sweet baby?" Lori asked as soon as
she entered the room. Who would have guessed that
beneath the awkward ugly duckling of high school lay

the makings of an all-American knockout? "She didn't hurt herself, did she?"

"No worse than any other day," Meg said, pouring her coffee. She'd never gotten around to touching the pot she'd made at home. "A bump on her noggin, but she was laughing with Rosemary when I left."

"Such a sweetheart," Lori said, and Meg had to wonder if her friend even realized the way she drew her hands to her stomach. But Meg noticed...and Meg knew. Lori and Trey had been trying for a baby for over five years. Recently they'd begun tests to figure out why they'd been unsuccessful.

"How's Trey?" she asked.

"Fine," Lori said with an odd briskness. Once, she would have smiled and launched straight into her latest Trey story. Now she again changed the subject. "I'm so glad you found someone to watch Char at your place."

Meg saw no point in pushing. The pace was Lori's to set. "Rosemary's a godsend," she agreed. A friend of her mother's, the former schoolteacher was itching for grandkids—and happy to practice with Charlotte.

"Oh." Lori put a dainty little mug with a Pisces sign on it into the sink. "That guy called for you again."

Meg looked up from the sugar packet she'd just opened. "The same one from yesterday? Did he say what he wanted?"

"Nope." Lori frowned. "Wouldn't leave a message or a name—but he had a great voice."

"Did you get his number?" Julia asked.

"Came in as Out-of-Area."

Julia's eyes took on a rare twinkle. "You hiding something, cuz?"

Meg dumped the sugar into her coffee. "I wish." It

had been a long time since there had been anything worth keeping to herself, certainly nothing in the man department.

With sobering speed, Julia became all business again, reaching into her blazer pocket. "Then here," she said, handing Meg a square, pink sheet of message paper.

"What's this?"

Julia's eyes, all steely and serious, met hers. "His number."

Meg stilled. Her throat burned. Something in her gut jumped. She didn't need to see the number to know that the subject of their conversation had shifted. Whereas Meg preferred to let sleeping dogs lie, Julia was all about meeting them head-on.

"I called the bureau," she said. "He's in Venezuela."

Against the thin paper, Meg's thumb and forefinger tightened.

"They said he's out on assignment, but they expect him back—"

"No." But Meg glanced at the string of fifteen numbers anyway. A phone number, such a simple thing really. Dial the numbers, hear the voice.

His voice.

I'm here…with you, he'd promised.

"Meg, you can't pretend he doesn't exist."

He'd said something almost identical right before he walked out the door: *I can't stay here anymore, can't pretend.*

Why didn't anyone understand there was a difference between prevention and pretending?

"I told you to leave it alone," Meg said, looking up.

But Julia wouldn't back down. She'd been on Meg

about this for almost two months, since shortly after the car accident that changed so many lives. "Russ was her brother."

Meg told herself to walk away. To wad up the paper and toss it in the garbage, go back to her office and prepare the agenda for the staff meeting or read Henry's report. Review plans for the silent auction, which she was in charge of.

But something inside her just broke.

"A lot of good that did her!" she snapped in a rare display of emotion. "He didn't even come for her funeral!" Didn't call to check on arrangements for her child, didn't acknowledge in any way, shape or form that the little sister who'd picked up her life in Scotland and traveled all the way to Texas, to be with her big brother, had died, here in a country so far removed from her family. Alone. Except for Meg—and Charlotte.

"Maybe he didn't find out in time." Lori's words were quiet, hopeful. A romantic down to the bone, she couldn't give up her belief in happy endings. Russell's rich brogue didn't help matters. In her book, just because he talked like a poet, he walked on water. "Maybe he couldn't."

"Of course he couldn't." Meg saw Lori wince, but it didn't change the truth. "Because that would have required him to come…" *Back.* Home. "Here." It still stunned Meg that someone Ainsley's age had actually made out a will. And that a nineteen-year-old from a small town in Scotland would choose to have her final resting place here in small-town America. Among strangers.

Of course, from what Meg knew of Ainsley's relationship with her parents, they, too, had become little more than strangers.

"Meg." Lori's voice was soft, pleading. "He's Charlotte's *uncle,* your—"

"Past." Meg swallowed hard, didn't want to hear the word. "He's my past, that's all."

Julia snatched the paper from Meg's fingers. "If you don't call him, I will."

The glare was automatic. Meg hated confrontation, but this wasn't a game or contest. It was real and it was absolutely none of Julia's business. *"Don't."*

She hated the way her voice broke on the word.

"Meg…" The lines of Julia's face softened. "It's not fair that you have to do this alone. Maybe he can help."

He. Him. Meg couldn't remember the last time any of them had spoken his name aloud. They didn't need to. They all knew.

"He *left,* Jules." Packed up, walked away. If she'd come home that night a little later, she still wondered if he would have said goodbye.

Just for a few weeks, a month at the most.

"You were going through a hard time," Julia reminded her. "You yourself said it was probably for the best."

She had. She'd said that in the immediate aftermath, when she'd found herself able to breathe for the first time in months.

But then the days piled onto one another, one after the other. And the nights…

"He didn't come back," she whispered. It was still almost unfathomable to her that the man she'd loved so dearly had turned his back on her so completely. He'd never called, sent only the occasional e-mail.

E-mail.

That's what their marriage had been reduced to.

"It's what he does." She still didn't understand how she'd been so blind. "What he always does." The pattern was clear now, time after time after time. He'd left his family the day he turned eighteen. He'd left the country of his birth. He'd left the news bureau, the university. "When the going gets tough…" Russell Montgomery walked.

But Julia wouldn't leave the subject alone. "Then why aren't you divorced?" Her tone made it sound like the answer was obvious.

"Just a technicality."

She lifted a perfectly sculpted brow. "That's a pretty big technicality."

Meg drew the mug to her mouth and took a sip of now-cool coffee. "It doesn't mean anything."

"Then why haven't you been with anyone else? Two years is a *long* time."

A strangled noise broke from Meg's throat. "What is this? Let's Ambush Meg Day?" Simply because Russell's parents had been calling and she hadn't called them back yet? She was going to. She had to. She knew that. So long as she was raising their granddaughter she couldn't pretend they didn't exist.

But not yet.

Done with it all, she snatched the paper from Julia and strode toward the door. "Editorial in ten," she called over her shoulder. Then, at the door, she turned. "And anyway," she tossed with a wicked little smile. "Who says I haven't?"

THE LATE-AFTERNOON SUN poured down, creating a stark contrast between the field and the impossible blue of the horizon. As far as the eye could see, red and yellow and blue swayed with the warm breeze.

"We're nearing peak," Ray Blunt said. The longtime Pecan Creek photographer slung his camera strap over his shoulder and reached into his pickup for his tripod. "Barring rain, we should be about perfect."

It was April in East Texas. Going without rain was about as likely as going without allergies.

"A little sprinkle won't hurt anyone," Meg said. It was the lightning she worried about, hail the size of tennis balls. One round of that and the carefully tended flower fields would be pulverized, destroying one of the big draws of the Wildflower Festival: photographs.

"Thanks for coming out with me," Ray said, taking a swig from his water bottle. He and her mother had been friends for as long as Meg could remember. Twisting for the baby, Meg grinned. Lately, she was pretty sure her mother and Ray's friendship involved some new... benefits.

"Just want to do one last dry run," he said. "Your mama thought your little girl would make a perfect guinea pig, if'n you don't mind me usin' that expression."

Your little girl...

Briskly Meg unfastened Charlotte from the car seat and shifted her onto her hip. She'd found the perfect frilly white dress.

"Here she is," she cooed, and with one three-toothed smile, Charlotte innocently chased Meg's worries away.

The three of them made their way from the gravel parking area as another car turned off the narrow highway. Meg pushed Charlotte in her new jogging stroller, navigating the winding trail as they went. Every year the town seeded the big field, making sure that with spring a colorful parade of bluebonnets and Indian paintbrush and poppies stood ready for the festival. Three years before they'd added irrigation to compensate for increasingly dry winters.

It was a photographer's paradise. Russell had once said—

Russell had said a lot of things.

"Just over yonder," Ray said, leading them down a small trail toward a monstrous patch of eager bluebonnets, dotted by the occasional red of a poppy. In the center, a small indentation marked the spot.

"Lighting is almost perfect," Ray observed while Meg lifted Charlotte from the stroller. They had the field all to themselves, except for the tall man in the distance. Against the Western sky the sun cast him in silhouette, but did nothing to hide the slight limp. "I've gotten some of my best shots this time of day. Just put her right…there."

Looking away from the stranger, Meg carried Charlotte through the flowers, trying not to crush any as she went. At the clearing, she smoothed Charlotte's fancy dress and lowered her toward the ground.

Charlotte started to cry.

"Oh, baby," Meg murmured, pulling back to look down at Charlotte's sweet little face—now red and splotchy. "No, no, no," she said, trying again.

But Charlotte wrapped her pudgy little arms around Meg's neck and clung on for dear life. "Mamamama…"

At a loss, Meg glanced back to the photographer who'd once taken similar pictures of her, when she was a child. To this day, they lined the hallway of the small ranch-style house in which she'd grown up. "This might take a while."

With a hand to his graying beard, her mother's *friend* shrugged. "Not a problem."

"Here now," she said to the baby. "Let Ma—" She broke off, tried again. "We can sit together," she said, rubbing her hand along Charlotte's back as she lowered her into the small clearing.

Honeybees buzzed up—and Charlotte's wails turned into shrieks.

"Tell you what," Ray said. "You take your time and I'm going to go get a picture of them poppies over there. When I come back, I'll get the two of you."

"No—I—" But he was already shuffling down the path. And anyway, Meg knew it was no use. She could tell the photographer she didn't want to be in any pictures, but he would take them anyway.

"That's my girl," she said, holding Charlotte close to her heart and rocking with the breeze. "There's nothing to be afraid of."

The baby nestled closer, much as she did during the stillness of the night. Sometimes they'd sit in the rocking chair with lullabies drifting through the room until the first rays of dawn filtered through the blinds. Sometimes Meg would fall asleep holding her. Lately, she'd begun carrying Charlotte back to her bed and snuggling up with her. Sleeping with a baby still worried her a little, but she was pretty sure Char was big enough and strong enough to scoot away if she needed to.

"See, it's all okay," she soothed, as she'd done for the past two months. She'd been there the morning Charlotte was born. She'd made a promise before God the day Charlotte was baptized. She'd held her and loved her, bathed her, dressed her, spoiled her madly.

But she'd never imagined that one day she would

hold a sleeping angel, while Father O'Sullivan read Charlotte's mother her last rites.

Meg closed her eyes and held her niece tight. The warmth of the sun felt good, the whisper of the breeze. The softness of the baby in her arms. For so long she'd wanted to share her life with a child.

But not like this.

Gradually Charlotte quit squirming, her body relaxing into the heaviness of sleep. Meg smiled, realizing once again that best-laid plans were the stuff of Lori's fairy tales.

Opening her eyes, she squinted against the glare of the late-afternoon sun and looked for Ray. She'd need to tell him—

At the edge of the clearing a lone man stood in the shade of a tall, gnarled post oak. The play of shadows stole detail, but still she knew. Two years could change a lot. Give, and take. Create, and devastate.

But they'd done nothing to mute the low quickening, the visceral reaction she'd first experienced one crisp fall day in New York a lifetime ago. He'd come into the lecture hall as a guest lecturer for her News Editorial class.

He'd walked out with her heart.

Now he stood not fifty feet away, the man who'd pulled into the parking lot as she and Charlotte had walked away, the man she'd seen at the edge of the clearing, watching. The low-slung jeans and wrinkled button-down were just as she remembered.

The limp was new.

CHAPTER TWO

Two and a half years before

"MEG, YOU READY?"

She looked up from the well-worn parenting magazine and grinned. Instinctively her hand slid to her tummy. "Absolutely."

Dr. Brennan's smile was warm. A tall, slender woman nearing sixty, she'd taken care of Meg since her first ob-gyn appointment over a decade before. "I thought Russell would be here."

Meg refused to let the frown form. Not today. "So did I," she admitted with a quick glance at her watch. She'd been leaving messages for half an hour. He'd yet to call her back. "He must have gotten hung up at a meeting."

It wasn't the first time, and, she figured, it wouldn't be the last. Russell was like that, always losing himself in one project or another. His mother called it escape, but Meg thought that was overly harsh. Russell was an intensely intense man. He did nothing halfway. He was all in, or all out.

"Should we wait a little bit?" Dr. Brennan asked. "I can probably spot you another fifteen or twenty minutes."

It was the right thing to do. Over the years he'd been

by her side at so many appointments and procedures. Rarely did he miss. But today...

"Nah," Meg said, standing. There was no telling how much longer Russell would be, and as it was, she'd been waiting just about her whole life for this. She could tell him the news herself. She could surprise him. She already had the pink and blue booties purchased.

After the sonogram, she'd know which pair to wrap.

"Let's do this," she said, reaching for her satchel.

Dr. Brennan nodded. "If you're sure," she said, escorting Meg toward the exam room. "Do you have any feelings, one way or the other?"

"Russell thinks girl."

"And you?"

"Healthy," Meg replied as a little flutter quaked through her. "I'm just thinking healthy."

Present Day

TWO YEARS WAS A LONG TIME.

Russell Montgomery stood on the edge of the field of blue, as much an outsider as the night he'd walked out the front door of the house that had quit being a home. He'd told himself not to look back. It wasn't healthy. Life was ahead of you, not behind.

His eyes had shifted to the rearview mirror anyway, for one last look. Of the cheery blue century-old house. Of the yard that sloped down to the lazy creek, the row of willows, weeping.

Of her.

Instead, he'd found clay pots with wilted flowers, a swing in need of repair, an empty porch and the truth.

There was nothing to look back at.

But forward... Forward had taken him far, given him much. In the primitive villages of Mozambique, the tight, poisonous coil inside him had loosened. There, he'd been able to breathe. With the passing of each day, all those dark, festering emotions that had chased him from Pecan Creek faded a little more, until all that remained was the clinical realization that the life he and Meg had been creating had been an illusion.

He'd never planned to come back.

Hell, who was he kidding? He'd never planned anything that had happened since the day Meg first walked into his world.

Africa was a continent of extremes, breathtaking beauty and mind-numbing depravity, lush jungles and barren deserts, kindness and cruelty.

Innocence.

Savagery.

Being back in America...in Pecan Creek...

It was like stepping back into an old, faded dream, familiar but fuzzy, fleeting but somehow ever seductive. You knew you were going to wake up, but for that briefest of moments, you wanted to just...linger.

She sat there among the army of bluebonnets, the warm April wind whipping wheat-colored hair against an oval face that had once dominated his dreams. The angles were the same, the wide cheekbones and tilted eyes. The mouth that had once been so quick to—

She wasn't smiling now. Her hair was longer than before, looser. The shield of flowers hid her clothes, but he could make out a trace of something dark—and a whole lot of skin.

And the baby...

Something hard and sharp sliced through him. He'd

seen a lot during his time away. He'd seen mothers and children, birth and death. But the sight of that chubby-cheeked little girl in Meg's lap, the frilly white dress and shot of bright red hair…

His bad leg throbbed. And for one brutal moment, everything between them fell away, the flowers and the years, the tears and the broken promises, leaving only him and Meg…and the baby they'd lost.

With eyes of blue like her mum's, he'd predicted.

Even now, the urge to pound his fist into something hard and unmovable ripped through him.

Slowly she rose from the bed of bluebonnets, easing the child to her chest. Sleeping, he realized. His sister's baby was sleeping.

Ainsley.

He still couldn't believe she was gone.

And that he was here.

And Meg was walking toward him. Meg of the pretty floral dresses, now wearing camouflage cargo pants and a black top that left little to his imagination.

Or his memory.

The urge to reach for his camera was pure instinct, the desire to capture the vivid contrast between innocence and—

He didn't know what. Typical Meg, she kept that all shuttered away, locked deep, deep inside, where no one could reach her.

No one could touch her.

Especially not him.

He didn't have his camera, but knew he didn't need it. Some images had a way of lasting all by themselves.

In the distance, old man Ray Blunt shuffled back into view. He paused and lifted a hand to his brow, watched.

The automatic wave surprised Russell. He'd always liked Ray, had learned a lot about the world from a man who'd never left Texas.

Ray returned the gesture, even though Russell was pretty sure the old man had no idea who he was.

But Meg did. She moved toward him, her stride strong and confident, her chin high, allowing the breeze to keep playing with the tangled strands of her hair. The longer length made her look younger than the last time he'd seen her.

Or maybe that was the baby sprawled all over her chest.

He was a man used to watching, to standing on the sidelines and documenting. Never get involved. That was how you stayed intact. But he started toward her anyway, acutely aware that he was not in Pecan Creek as a journalist.

Narrow trails of mutilated bluebonnets wound through the flowers. Once he'd chosen his steps carefully. Now he let instinct guide him—and kept his eyes trained forward.

On the woman he left behind.

IN THE BEGINNING, she'd imagined this. During those first few weeks and months, she'd closed her eyes and seen him walking toward her, that pure, undiluted focus in the bottomless green of his eyes, the...longing. Sometimes he would walk in through the back door. Sometimes he would find her sitting by the young willow they'd planted near the creek bed.

Once she'd seen him at the edge of the cemetery.

It was always the same. She would stand. He would approach. Arms were opened. She stepped in. Words weren't spoken.

Words weren't needed.

Only Russell.

Now…God…now. Her chest tightened. Her throat burned. Beyond him she saw her car, but knew there was no way to reach the Lexus without getting by him.

Russell Montgomery was back in Pecan Creek.

"Meggie," he said as the distance between them narrowed, and something inside her screamed. The last fringes of the dream shattered, even as the whisper of a different dream echoed through her.

Two years. Two years since she'd heard the rolling lilt of her own husband's voice.

"And this must be little Charlotte," he commented with the polite formality of a complete stranger. "She looks—"

"Don't." The word burned on the way out. Meg stopped and looked up at him, could do nothing about the hot boil moving through her. "You don't get to say that."

Russell stopped moving. "Meggie, look, I understand—"

"You don't understand a thing." Meg barely recognized the rasp to her own voice. It had been almost ten weeks since the insanely clear February day when they'd buried this man's sister…ten weeks during which he'd been conspicuously silent. No way could he just stroll back into town and say hello, make some kind of inane remark about who Charlotte looked like. *"She was your sister, Russell.* She deserved better."

So had Meg.

The lines of his face went tight. "You know that's not how I meant it," he said, and she made herself swallow.

"I just… Christ, Meg, I don't know what you want me to do."

Hadn't that always been the problem?

"This isn't about me," she said automatically. It wasn't about them. "It's about Ainsley. She *worshipped* you, Russell. Thought you hung the moon. And yet you couldn't even be bothered to come say goodbye."

"I didn't know."

That stopped her. She shifted the baby, careful to keep one hand against the back of Charlotte's head. "Didn't know what? That Ainsley loved you? Why else would she have left Scotland to come live with us?"

Only a few clouds drifted across the blue sky, but the shadows about Russell deepened. "That she died."

The quiet stillness to his voice went through Meg like broken glass.

"I didn't know that she died until two weeks ago."

"I called your parents." Had called him first, from the hospital moments after Dr. Harrison had given her the horrible news. Instinctively she'd reached for her phone and called Russell, held her breath while the phone rang.

Froze when she got his voice mail.

She'd stood there in the starkly lit Emergency Room in the hour before dawn, listening. To his voice. His warm, casual message. But the beep had brought everything back into cruel, sharp focus, and she'd ended the call and swallowed hard, annoyed that after all this time, despite the divorce papers she'd had drawn up the month before, he'd been the first one she'd thought of.

Because Ainsley was his sister, she'd realized. Meg had loved her dearly, but in the end, it was Russell's blood that flowed through Ainsley's veins.

And Charlotte's.

He stood there now, a tall man with a body that promised strength, even as an unmistakable mist clouded his eyes.

"I was on assignment," he said in a voice so stripped down Meg had to concentrate to hear him. "My parents decided to wait until I was back before telling me."

She couldn't stop her mouth from dropping open. "Why would they do that?" she asked. "Because they didn't want to inconvenience you? She was their child. She deserved…" The words trailed off as the memories edged closer. The knock at the door. The race to the hospital. Ainsley on the bed, the tubes and machines, the punishing sense of urgency as everyone seemed to move in slow motion.

"I would have come, Meggie. If I'd known, I would have been here."

A fresh wave of grief surged up from that deep, dark place, burning her throat anew. For Ainsley, she told herself. Not because of the sound of her name in her husband's voice. No one else had ever called her Meggie.

No one else had ever made her name sound like a caress.

And for that, she hated him.

"No one was here," she said, still stung by how wrong it had been. "No one from your family. None of her friends." Not even Charlotte's father. Only Meg and Julia and Lori, a handful of locals. "She deserved better than that."

Russell's jaw tightened. "I'm glad she had you," he said. "That's why she stayed, you know."

After he left.

"I wasn't family."

Russell frowned. "Meggie...you know that's not true."

She looked away, toward the honeybees buzzing around her ankles. Meg had always wanted a sister. She had two cousins in town, but it wasn't the same. Julia and Faith had lived in a big two-story house in a nice subdivision and took exotic vacations...with both their parents.

Meg had never even known her father.

Then Ainsley had come to town shortly after Meg and Russell married, a troubled teenager with a rebellious streak as long as a hot summer day, and a heart as tender as a dewdrop. After Russell left—

Meg looked back up, felt something inside her shift. His smile was soft and warm, gentle. *Sad*. The lines of his face had relaxed, even the perpetual five o'clock shadow looked softer. But it was his eyes that got her, the crinkling at the corners, the warmth of the green, the glow of discovery and vulnerability.

Meg's hold on Charlotte tightened. She glanced down to find the baby awake, her big eyes trained curiously on the uncle she'd never met.

"Well, hello there, poppet," he murmured in the dialect of his childhood, and Charlotte's little mouth lifted into a delighted smile.

Meg wanted to wake up.

But knew that this was no dream.

"There's my girl," she said, shifting Charlotte so that she rode Meg's hip. "What a good little nap you had."

Russell kept staring, as if the baby might vanish if he so much as took his eyes off her. "She's—"

"Wonderful," Meg finished for him. A bittersweet gift she'd never expected. "She's got so much of Ainsley in her." And Russell. His eyes. His smile.

His infectious laugh.

At first being around Charlotte had hurt. But there'd been no one else to step in. Ainsley had never tried to track down her daughter's father, saying only that he couldn't be with them.

"Then she must not be sleeping much," Russell said, and before she could stop herself, Meg laughed.

She didn't want to laugh.

"Fits and starts," she said. Insomnia had been Ainsley's middle name. Rumor had it she'd had her days and nights mixed up from the time she was born. "But we're working on it."

"Ainsley always said—" Russell broke off, lifting a hand to feather a finger along the underside of Charlotte's foot.

She giggled.

"Always said what?" Meg asked.

"That she wanted to be a mum."

Meg closed her eyes. That was true. Piercings, tattoos, wild streak and all, even at nineteen, Ainsley had been a great mother. It just takes love, she'd said. Just… love.

"And so did you."

The quiet words did cruel, cruel things to Meg's heart. She opened her eyes and stepped back. Away. Couldn't imagine anything she wanted less than to be standing in a field of bluebonnets making polite small talk with the husband she had not seen in two years.

"Your mother's been calling." And now Russell stood before her, a stranger in a painfully familiar body. The eyes…the mouth. The thick copper hair. As always, his shirt was open at the throat, revealing a hint of the dark springy hair she'd once loved to finger. Just to the right, she knew there would be a scar. "Is that why you're here?"

The change was immediate. His flirty little Charlotte-inspired smile congealed into something harder—and much less readable. His gaze turned serious, and on a visceral level, Meg started to scream.

No.

She'd always known this day could come. Ainsley had left a will, but wills could be challenged. Technically, she was the outsider. If the Montgomery family was to challenge her for custody, she had a horrible feeling she knew what the outcome would be.

"Actually, it is," Russell said, and as if a switch had been flicked, the lilt left his voice. "My parents wanted me to come and—"

Meg shifted to get a better grip on a suddenly squirmy baby.

"—settle Ainsley's affairs."

The breeze kept whispering. The bees kept buzzing. A few cars sped along the narrow highway. But Meg held herself very still. "Settle her affairs?" Her voice was barely more than a rasp.

Russell's eyes met hers. Once, in what seemed like another lifetime, she'd known his every look, touch. Words had been a formality they'd rarely needed.

She'd never imagined how quickly silence could turn to poison.

Or how badly it could punish.

After he'd left, at first the days had been so much better. But the nights…

The nights had been another story.

And now they were reduced to awkward formalities. There was a searching in his gaze, the photojournalist hard at work, studying, analyzing. Seeking. And in response, she tucked all those nasty, tattered remnants away, unwilling to give him a story to work with. Two years was a long time. A lot had happened. Not all of it would please a judge.

The last thing she needed was award-winning journalist Russell Montgomery on a fact-finding mission.

His eyes narrowed, as if he was squinting against a bright glare. "Her house," he said as Charlotte started to thwack her hand against Meg's chest. "Her belongings."

Caution prevented relief from stirring. "Everything's still there. I…" Had been to the house the day Ainsley died only long enough to gather a few essentials for the baby. The next day, Lori's husband, Trey, had brought over the crib and glider, the rest of Charlotte's toys and clothes.

Meg had been unable to go back since.

"Between the paper and the Wildflower Festival I haven't had a chance to sort through everything yet." In truth, there wasn't much. Ainsley had worked as a waitress. Funds had been tight. She'd been so excited when one of her customers had offered her the use of his mother's vacant house. "Julia and Lori offered to help me, but it just doesn't seem to happen."

Probably because a very strong part of her wasn't ready for that kind of closure.

"I understand," Russell said, and from the thickness of his voice, she knew that he did. No matter what had gone down between the two of them, he'd always had a soft spot for his sister. "I don't want to be here, either."

Somehow she didn't wince. She kept her expression blank, her voice neutral. "Come by the paper tomorrow," she said as Charlotte tugged at the collar of her shirt. She nuzzled in, her mouth open and seeking.

Russell's eyes followed, the green quickly taking on a dark glitter she'd worked hard to forget.

The quickening was immediate—and the final straw. Meg shifted the hungry baby from her chest and lowered her to stand on top of her own feet, Char's chubby little legs wobbling like gelatin.

"I've got the keys there," Meg said as if nothing had just happened. The baby clutching her fingers for dear life, she glanced back at Russell.

He looked as though he'd seen a ghost.

"A day or two tops," she said, "and then you can be on your way."

A harsh sound broke from his throat…the same sound he always made when he didn't know what to say. "Is she walking?"

"Not yet," Meg said, easing her right foot forward. "At least, not by herself." Then, to the baby, "Such a big, strong girl!"

Charlotte giggled as if she understood. She leaned forward, urging Meg to keep moving.

Meg obliged.

"Ray's back."

Meg looked up. "What?"

Russell gestured behind her, where her mother's friend stood alongside the swarm of bluebonnets where he'd first tried to take Charlotte's picture.

"Oh, good," she said, turning to start back. "Maybe this time we can actually get some pictures." She wasn't sure what made her twist toward Russell. He hadn't moved a muscle, stood there as still as one of the old post oaks surrounding the field, watching.

And then she got it. The baby. *His sister's child.*

Charlotte was the spitting image of Ainsley, who was the spitting image of Russell. Seeing her *was* like seeing a ghost. Sometimes Meg still couldn't believe her sister-in-law was gone.

"Here," she said before thinking. She lifted her arms, bringing the giggling baby up toward her uncle. "You want to hold her?"

CHAPTER THREE

Two and a half years before

PINK BALLOONS BOBBED against the passenger window, straining to get free. Twelve of them, including a Mylar in the shape of little booties. The tulips lay on the front seat, beside the grape juice.

She was going to be upset. Russell knew that. She wasn't even answering his calls. He'd tried to get away, but the meeting ran long, and as usual, he lost track of time.

Frowning, he was turning onto the narrow road that led to their house when he remembered to check his messages. He hadn't checked before, hadn't wanted to hear the news that way. He'd wanted to see her face, her smile. He'd wanted to be there.

Now, almost home, he wondered if she was somewhere else.

Five messages waited. The first three were hang-ups. The fourth was a former colleague. Finally, with the fifth, he heard her voice, and his heart started to slam.

"Honey…" Meg was a confident woman, vivacious, full of energy and life. But now… "I…I…" She never stuttered. She never stammered. "I…"

The sickness hit fast, spreading like a toxin in his gut.

"We need to talk," she said, sounding so very, very far away. So small. "Come home…please."

He was barely aware of his foot ramming down on the gas pedal, racing the last of the way home. He swerved into the driveway and threw open the door, strode toward the house. The balloons were in his hand. The tulips were not.

"Meg?" he called as he opened the door.

The shadows of early afternoon greeted him. There were no lights turned on. No music. "Meggie?"

The stillness deepened with every step he took. The kitchen, the family room, the bedroom—the nursery. All empty.

"Meggie!"

He didn't know why he started to run. Everything was spinning…inside. Outside. Throwing open the back door, he squinted against the sun—and saw her.

And then everything stopped.

She was just sitting there. Down by the creek, with her back against one of the old weeping willows. Her knees were drawn to her chest. Her arms were wrapped around them. Her gaze was trained forward, toward the slow trickle of water in the creek.

On the breeze, he heard the choked sound of crying.

He staggered, started to run again. He thought he called out to her, but his throat was raw and she didn't turn. She sat there, frozen.

And God help him, he knew.

His steps slowed as the sprawl of green grass down to the creek stretched. Numbly, his hand, clenching the tangle of pink ribbons, went slack, and the bobbing mass of balloons lifted toward the blue of the sky.

And floated away.

Present Day

THE RAW, NAKED EMOTION on Russell's face congealed into something unreadable. "No. I—I can't hold her... right now." He ripped his gaze from the baby, backed away.

From his own niece.

"Ray's waiting," he said. "I—I'll be by in the morning."

And with that he turned and headed back to the sporty blue rental waiting in the gravel parking lot.

Meg wanted to be surprised. Angry. She was neither. Backing away, walking away, that's what Russell Montgomery did.

The hurt and disappointment were for Charlotte. She was just a baby, an innocent in all this. She deserved better. But as Meg carried her niece through a patch of poppies, toward Ray, the pressure in her chest released, and once again, she could breathe.

Russell had talked of Ainsley's affairs, of her house and her belongings...but not of her baby. He didn't even want to hold her.

And if he didn't hold her, he couldn't take her.

TIME DIDN'T STAND STILL. Russell knew that. It's just the way it was, a simple fact he'd always appreciated. In the two years since he'd last driven the shady streets of Pecan Creek, a child had been born, a bright light extinguished, a marriage ended.

But as he steered his rental car beneath a banner advertising the annual Wildflower Festival, it was like driving straight back into a past he knew no longer existed.

The cobblestone streets and old-time storefronts of

the historic district welcomed him, just as they welcomed everybody. Park benches sat beneath awnings. Nostalgic statues stood by the street corners. Even the old gazebo still waited there in the Side Street Park, if possible a brighter white than the last time he'd seen it.

The storefronts were the same, even if some of the names had changed. The old antiques shop was now a tearoom. The independent bookseller now boasted CDs and DVDs, as well. On the outskirts of town he'd noticed the big antebellum house turned bed-and-breakfast had a grand-reopening sign hung out front. Once, the renowned Magnolia Manor had attracted visitors from all across the country.

Russell wondered how long it had been closed.

Easing along the busy street that cut the town in half, he strained against the shadows of late afternoon for the familiar green awning across from the *Gazette*. He'd eaten at five-star restaurants in more major cities than he could count, but all it took was the thought of Uncle Ralph's, and his mouth started to water. If the local favorite was gone—

It wasn't. The hole-in-the-wall sat where it always had, tucked between Ed's Barber Shop and Dr. Harrison's office. There was almost always a crowd milling around out front, waiting for one of the ten tables inside.

At least, that's how many tables had been there before.

Russell had talked to Uncle Ralph about expanding or relocating, but the sole proprietor had always resisted, saying he couldn't cook for more than ten tables at a time, so why seat more than ten at a time?

Easing into a parallel spot across the street, Russell

couldn't help but smile at the memory. Once and only once, he'd suggested that Uncle Ralph hire someone to help...

Once. Only once.

Now he made his way across the street, glancing at his phone to check the time, when he noticed no one lingering out front. A few minutes past seven. He would have expected a crowd.

At the door, he wasn't sure why he hesitated. He'd eaten at the restaurant more times than he could count. He and Meg had come here frequently, sometimes several times per week. After work they'd walk over, sometimes just the two of them, often with Lori and Julia. The guys would arrive shortly thereafter. It had been their ritual.

Stepping back inside...

He almost turned and walked away, toward the new place down the street, Mamacitas. Instead he yanked open the door and strode into the restaurant lit by dozens of strings of festive chili pepper yard lights.

He saw them immediately, all of them, Julia and Lance and Lori and Trey. It was hard not to. His gaze went straight to their booth, the big curved one in the back right corner where they all used to sit and see who could throw back the most tequila shots. Once Meg had—

He turned to leave.

The sharp intake of breath was the only warning he got. "Rusty Montgomery!" Before he could turn—or run for the door—Ralph's wife was across the room. "As I live and breathe," she cried as she took him by the arm and beamed up at him. "Lord o'mercy *it is* you!"

And then it was all he could do not to choke on the heavy scent of gardenia—and grease. Ruby wrapped him up tight in her beefy arms, hugging him as if she'd never thought to see him again.

"I never thought this day would come," she said when she finally released him. "You done broke my heart when you left like that, without even coming to tell me bye."

By now everyone in the whole restaurant was watching—including the foursome at the back booth. Russell wanted the floor to just open up and swallow him, but since that wasn't going to happen, he opted for Plan B.

"Ruby Rodriguez," he said, rolling his *R*s. "Still as pretty as the day is long."

Her smile widened, but the glint in her eyes told him she knew what he was trying to do. "Go on with you now," she said, gesturing toward the familiar booth. "Your friends are waiting."

The words were casual enough, but they hit him like a rock to the gut. A big one. The foursome didn't move, just watched, leaving the ball square in Russell's court.

Until Lance stood. "Rusty," his former poker buddy said, crossing to him with a hand outstretched. There was a quiet understanding in his voice—and a steely warning in his eyes. "Didn't know you were back in town, man."

Trey was there a step later, and as Russell extended his hand, the man he'd once run with almost every morning before the sun rose wrapped him in a quick hug. The gesture caught him by surprise…but nowhere near as much as the realization that his friend had lost a lot of weight.

Trey released him abruptly, as if just realizing what he'd done. "When did you get back?"

"This morning," Russell said. "Need to clean out—"

"No, you don't." That was Julia. He'd wondered how long it would take the barracuda to march over. "There's nothing you need to do here," she said, angling her chin in that fierce way of hers.

Her husband looked as if he, too, wanted the floor to swallow him. "Julia—"

"No," Meg's cousin said before Lance could get out another word. She lifted her hand in a sharp gesture. "He doesn't get to do this." She kept her eyes trained on her prey, namely Russell. "You can't just show up here like…you still belong."

He blinked. Julia had always been a bull-by-the-horns kind of gal, but her vehemence seemed a little over-the-top. "Ainsley was my sister—"

"And Meg was your *wife*." She practically spat the word at him. "That didn't seem to make any difference, did it? You still walked away. You don't get to—"

"Jules." Lori materialized by her friend's side with an icy glare as she laid a hand to Julia's forearm. "Don't."

Something dark and uncomfortable slipped through Russell. He'd known coming back would not be easy, but the palpable tension among the foursome drove home just how long he'd been gone—and how much he didn't know. Trey was rail thin. Lori looked sad, drawn. Lance looked fed up. And Julia…Julia looked like she wanted to bust some balls.

Namely, his.

"I don't get to do what?" he asked.

Lori looked down. Julia's mouth pursed into a thin line. But it was Trey who spoke. "Come on, that was a long time ago," he said to his wife and her friend. "It

wasn't a picnic for anyone. When a marriage ends…"
He lifted a hand to rub at his chest, but left the rest of
his sentence unspoken.

But Russell knew. When a marriage ended, it was
like a death. But the kicker was, you both still lived. You
lived, while every other aspect of your life—where you
lived, what you did, who you did it with, *your freaking
identity*—went away.

Once those in Meg's inner circle had considered Russell a friend, and he them. They'd worked together,
laughed together, cried together. Now at best he was a
stranger. At worst…an enemy.

Not surprisingly, it was Lori who broke the awkward
silence. "Have you seen her?"

A photojournalist, Russell was a man who dealt in
images. Some he captured with film. Others imprinted
themselves on him, lingering long, long after time had
moved on. When he closed his eyes, it was a veritable
slide show of his life.

Since returning to Pecan Creek, that slide show was
of Meg.

"This afternoon," he said, feeling his chest tighten
all over again. In a perfect world, he could have slipped
in and out of town without seeing her. Christ, he could
have avoided coming back altogether.

But it wasn't a perfect world, and he could not do
what had to be done without involving her.

"At the flower field," he murmured as an after-
thought. "She had the baby.…"

Julia and Lori exchanged a quick glance. Two minutes later they'd retrieved their purses and were gone,
leaving the men standing in an awkward vortex of country music and silence.

STARS TWINKLED throughout the shadowy nursery, blue shimmers of light courtesy of the funky projector in the center of the room. Beatles music turned lullabies drifted from the CD player on the dresser. It was the perfect atmosphere for sleeping, but Charlotte, despite being bathed, lotioned and fed, had absolutely no interest in sleeping.

Still Meg rocked, cradling the chubby baby in her arms as she watched the numbers on the clock slip deeper into the evening.

"What a good day you had," she cooed, even though Charlotte was focused on the pile of blocks she'd been playing with earlier.

Meg wasn't about to allow her back down on the floor. This was attempt number three at sleep. There would not be a fourth.

"Posing so pretty for Uncle Ray," she went on in the same monotone. The second time had been the charm. Rejuvenated from her power nap, Charlotte had sat happily in the big patch of bluebonnets, cheerfully destroying one flower at a time.

Ray said the pictures would be great.

Meg had to take his word for it, because in truth, she had no idea. She'd tried to watch. She'd tried to pay attention. But the image of Russell limping toward her had stayed with her long after he himself had vanished.

Even now, hours later, the reality of it all kept winding through her, tighter with each minute that passed. This is what it had been like before, back when they'd come home from work each day and pretended they had a marriage. When they'd shared a silent dinner before each retreating to their own space. When they'd lain in bed with their backs to each other, faking sleep.

And so much more.

With the memory, all those old sensations knotted inside her once again, bringing with them a renewed frustration. She and Charlotte were just settling into a routine. The paper was in trouble. Circulation was down, advertising almost cut in half. With more and more folks consuming their news from online sources, interest in dailies and weeklies was at an all-time low. If she didn't come up with a turnaround soon, the paper would go under.

She did not have time for Russell Montgomery to stroll back into town.

On a deep inhalation, she glanced down and found Charlotte's eyes heavy, slowly blinking. Exhaling, she stopped rocking and waited.

The baby's eyes drifted closed.

Still Meg sat in the rocking chair, looking down at Charlotte's sweet little face. Sometimes getting her to sleep was a bear, but those first few moments of slumber were worth the effort. The innocence of it all screamed through Meg, filling her with a soft determination that would have sent her to her knees had she not been sitting.

Charlotte. Poor sweet Charlotte. Ainsley had loved her so very, very much.

Meg closed her eyes against the memory, but images awaited in the darkness, as well. Ainsley on the hospital bed, weak, fading. Reaching for her baby one last time.

Inside, something started to shake. Fighting it, Meg reached for all those slip-sliding pieces and locked them away, stood and eased the baby into her crib. In the hall, she crossed to her office, but found herself heading for the kitchen instead. She just needed…

At the oven, she went up on her toes and opened the cabinet, saw the lone bottle. She'd put the five-year-old cabernet there the night after Charlotte was born. Maybe tonight was the night to allow herself just one glass....

Meg...where were ye? I was scared my wee one would get here before you did....

She closed the cabinet. Walked out of the kitchen. Back to her office. Shut the door.

That's where she was when her cell phone rang. She picked it up, answered on the second ring.

"Open up," Julia said by way of greeting.

Meg blinked. "Pardon?"

"We're on the porch," Julia said in that brisk, all-business way of hers. "Didn't want to knock and risk waking the baby."

Puzzled, Meg saved the business plan she'd been editing and went to the front of the house, where she opened the door to Julia and Lori, and a nondescript brown bag.

Julia brushed right by her, looking both ways as she crossed the small foyer. "Is he here? Is that his truck out front?"

Meg glanced out to see the white, late-model truck across the street. "Is who here?"

Lori stepped inside and closed the door. "We know," she said quietly. "We saw him."

Meg stilled as realization formed. Her friends had seen Russell. And here they were...checking on her.

Because they knew—everything.

"He's not here." The truck across the street had been there a few days, most likely belonging to one of Mrs. Morgan's grown sons. "And you don't need to be here, either. I'm fine."

"Right," Julia said. "Your husband waltzes back into town after *two years*—"

"Soon-to-be-ex," Meg corrected. She'd filed the papers the month before Ainsley had died. All they needed were his signature.

"My point exactly."

Lori's eyes widened as Julia whisked into the kitchen. "You should have seen her. She pretty much let him have it."

Meg sighed. "Julia!" Then, "What happened to *'You have to call him'*?"

Julia returned with three spoons. "Your terms," she said. "Not his."

It was hard to argue with that.

"And so you came over here to…?" she asked, glancing from the bag in Lori's hands to the utensils in Julia's.

Julia grinned. "Eat ice cream." Tucking her arm under Meg's, she all but dragged her to the back door.

Meg thought about protesting, telling them she was fine. Insisting that they go home. She hated that they felt the need to descend on her as if she was some fragile creature in danger of shattering.

But gratitude overrode everything else.

Over the years they'd shared a lot, from Barbie clothes to real clothes, and then real dreams. And real heartache. Julia and Lori had been there before she went off to college—and when Meg came home. They'd listened to her go on and on about the dreamy guest professor—and they'd gawked when he came after her. They knew about the night she lost her virginity. They'd helped her plan her wedding. They'd encouraged her when she and Russell had been forced to turn to medical science to conceive a child. They'd held her hand, helped with shots, held her up.

In the end, they'd been the ones to help glue all the pieces back together.

Outside, on the wide porch overlooking the yard that sloped down to the creek, she let them steer her to the top step, where they all three plopped down. Lori pulled the carton out of the bag. Julia ripped off the lid, revealing the mint chip ice cream beneath.

Lori handed over the spoons.

They all dug in.

THE *PINEY WOODS GAZETTE* had once been a thriving daily newspaper. Meg's great-grandfather had prided himself on being a newsman, founding the local paper to quiet the gossip that often gripped the town. He had been a man of facts. A man of principle. Focus. He thought everyone had a right to know…everything.

It was a legacy Maxwell Landry dedicated his life to building—and passing down to his only son.

Standing outside the offices of the *Gazette,* Russell figured it was probably best neither man had lived to see the newspaper business slowly wither away. More and more consumers were getting their news from alternative sources, particularly online. Print was static, cumbersome. Passé. It was only a matter of time before physical newspapers became a thing of the past. He and Meg had spent countless hours working on strategies—

He frowned. No strategy in the world could stop the continuum of change. You adapted, or you became obsolete.

He and Meg had never been very good at adapting. Neither had Ainsley. From the time she'd been just a toddler, his sister had never been able to just go with the flow. She'd seen the world through a lens all her own, and now she was gone.

It still hurt like hell.

Hating what had to be done, he pushed open the door and strode into the outer office, as he'd done hundreds of times before. And just like all those times before, the scent of vanilla and orange greeted him. His office had been down the hall to the left, across from Meg's. Sometimes he'd worked there, but more often than not, he'd roamed the vacant space upstairs. He could think better there, without walls everywhere he turned.

Lori sat at the front desk, flanked by two ficus trees. Her role had expanded beyond being a receptionist, but with limited budgets, staffing had become an issue— and someone needed to sit out front.

Lori, with her warm smile and inherent gentleness, was the obvious choice.

She looked up from her computer screen, and again, all Russell could think was how tired she looked. Dark smudges ringed her eyes, the glare of the overhead lights making her look even more pale. She and Meg were roughly the same age, which put her at thirtyish. But she looked far older.

"Hi," she greeted, and he couldn't help but smile. He'd always had a soft spot for Lori.

"Hi, yourself," he said. "You okay?"

She smiled, and the shadows seemed to recede. "Just tired," she said, downplaying his question. "Busy day ahead. Trey has an—" She broke off, shook her head. "You're here for Meg."

They were simple words…true. But not true at all. "I need to get the keys—"

She picked up a small retro Magic 8 Ball from beside

a picture frame on the edge of her desk. From it dangled two hot-pink keys. "Got 'em."

Lori had the keys. Meg had given them to her. Obviously she had no intention of seeing him.

The quick burn in his gut surprised him.

"I expected her back by now," Lori said, "but the festival meetings almost always run long."

With two long strides he was across the cozy reception area. He reached out, almost grabbed the keys. But this was Lori, not Meg, and she'd never been anything but kind to him. Jaw tight, he forced a smile and took the keys, made the requisite small talk before returning to his rental car.

How like Meg to avoid what she didn't want to face.

The drive across town took less than ten minutes. He pulled off the quiet crepe myrtle–lined boulevard and wound his way through a few side streets before arriving at the small frame house.

Flowers bloomed. Everywhere he looked, a rainbow of colors screamed back at him. Pink and white from the azaleas, red from geraniums, yellow from daisies and daffodils. Even the trees rained colors, a veritable parade of dogwood and redbuds, all shimmering in the late-morning sun like something straight out of a picture book.

Once he would have grabbed his camera and gone down on his knee, searching for the perfect blend of light and shadow and color. That's what Ainsley had always loved, the contrasts in life. The unexpected.

The house had been drab when she'd first showed it to him, gray in the dead of winter. He'd thought she was making a mistake, but she'd seen the promise, and she'd insisted.

Now she was gone, but the color remained.

Russell pushed the car door open and stepped into the seductive warmth of Texas in April. He was a man who thrived on the periphery, the complete opposite of his baby sister. No matter how much he did not want to go inside, he owed her. This, and a whole lot more.

Striding up the walk, he made his way between the armies of petunias lining the walkway, up the two steps to the screened porch, and yanked open the outer door.

Meg rose from the porch swing, the baby on her hip. "Hey," was all she said.

He stopped, stared at her standing there in a fall of sunlight, her jeans faded, her scoop-neck olive shirt wrinkled. Her hair was soft, loose.

"Meggie." Goddamn his voice for breaking.

She shifted little Charlotte on her hip. "Lori called, told me I'd just missed you."

His hand tightened around the key.

"My meeting ran over," she said as Charlotte fisted her hand in Meg's hair and yanked. "I must have been crazy signing up to chair. You wouldn't believe how many last-minute details there are."

The edges of the key dug into his palm. "You always were one for staying busy."

Her smile was lopsided, and with it about a thousand years fell away. "That's one way of putting it, I suppose."

The tension spun out between them, the stillness and the silence pushing in like invisible walls. Once he'd known this woman as well as he'd known himself, her body—her heart. Or at least, he'd thought he had. She'd been his wife and his friend, his coworker and confidante, his lover. They'd bought a falling-down house and turned it into a home. They'd shared meals and dreams, their bodies…

Now they stood in the cramped confines of the small front porch, without a freaking clue what to say to each other.

CHAPTER FOUR

Two and a half years before

THE HOUSE WAS QUIET. Not that long ago, the silence would have surprised him. Meg loved music. She always had it going, blasting so that she could hear it in every room. He would come home and find her doing the dishes to U2, dusting to The Boss, paying bills to Dave Matthews.

He'd never understood how she could concentrate with so much else going on.

She'd never understood how he could concentrate with what she called the scream of silence.

Now that silence filled the house. Once he would have called out to her, but now he moved quietly through the foyer. He didn't want her to know he was home. Not yet. There'd been a Web site launch meeting that afternoon at the *Gazette*—but she'd never showed. Lori said she'd gone out for coffee a little after two.

She'd never come back.

She did that a lot these days.

He found her in the kitchen, the big walk-in pantry to be exact. The navy suit she'd put on that morning was gone, replaced by a boxy T-shirt and baggy jeans. They literally hung on her. Her feet were bare, her hair loose.

The urge to—Russell didn't know. He didn't know

what he wanted to do—what he was supposed to do. Six weeks had passed since they'd lost their baby…a little girl. Dr. Brennan said Meg had recovered physically, but emotionally…

Julia said to give her time.

Meg's mother, Lilah, said to give her love.

Russell had tried both.

Now he watched her alphabetize their canned goods, and wanted to put his fist through the goddamn wall.

"Hey," he finally said.

She stiffened. His wife. She stiffened at the sound of his voice.

"Missed you this afternoon." He'd quit asking if she was okay.

Slowly she turned, looked at him with those awful, blank eyes of hers. "The pantry's driving me crazy."

He felt his jaw tighten, didn't have a clue what to say in response—she'd arranged the cans by size and color the week before. "Meggie—" He reached for her, stilled when he saw her wince.

His wife. Wincing because he wanted to touch her.

"I can finish up for you," he said. "Why don't you go ahead and shower."

She blinked at him. "Shower?"

"The play tonight," he reminded her. *Evangeline*— one of her favorites. "Lori and Trey will be by in about an hour. They want to stop by Uncle Ralph's first—"

Her eyes darkened. "No." It was barely more than a whisper.

"Sweetheart—"

But she was shaking her head, backing away. "Not tonight."

The very real dread in her eyes gutted him. "It's been six weeks," he said as gently as he could. Six weeks during which she'd hardly slept, eaten. She was lost behind a wall of grief, he knew, but he couldn't find so much as a crack to slip through. "They're your friends.…"

Her mouth went tight, and in the harsh glare of the fluorescent light, he saw how pale she'd become. How gaunt. The beautiful, soft swell from pregnancy…gone. Even the lines of her face were stark.

"Not tonight," she said, then turned back to the canned goods, picked up a damp rag and started to clean the already spotless shelf.

Present Day

OUTSIDE, WHERE NATURE provided the water, color rioted. Here on the screened porch, the profusion of clay pots in multiple sizes sat empty, save for a scraggle of pale green weeds.

Somehow Russell resisted the childish urge to kick one into about a thousand pieces. The question burning his throat was another story. "What are you doing here?"

As far as finesse went, he flat-out flunked. But it was better than the poison of silence.

There'd been so much of that.

Sunlight slanted through the branches of the century-old live oak in the front yard, casting Meg's face half in shadow, half in light. She pulled her lower lip in and bit down, reminding him of the girl he'd first seen almost a decade before, sitting in the front row of the lecture hall.

He'd already been a seasoned photojournalist. He'd covered war and famine and the kind of natural disasters that made you question…everything. He'd experienced luxury and poverty, sin and virtue, and everything in between. All the while he'd made himself walk through it all, objective, documenting rather than experiencing.

But this girl in the front row... She had wheat-colored hair, a glow in her exotically tilted eyes, an eagerness in her slightly parted lips. She'd watched him with a provocative combination of wholesomeness and determination.

Christ, after almost ten years, he could still feel the heat sear through him.

It was much the way she watched him now.

"I don't really know what I'm doing here," she said, answering his question with a candor that reminded him of that long-ago girl, the one who'd spoken honestly and passionately...who never ran and hid. She glanced at the big picture window to her right, then at the child in her arms.

His sister's child.

"I loved Ainsley, too." Her words were quiet, hoarse, and he had no doubt that they were absolutely true. "I owe her this," she said. "I promised..." She looked toward the scattering of empty pots for a long moment before lifting her eyes back to him. "I promised her I would take care of...everything. I can't turn my back now just because it's not easy."

Russell shifted, easing the weight from his right leg. If he stood too long without moving, the residual ache turned to more of a stab. His doc said it was phantom pain...but his hand found his thigh anyway, and rubbed.

And for the first time since he'd found out about Ainsley, he let himself think about what it must have been like for Meg. He'd been so insulated from her, had trained himself not to think of her, that he'd thought of nothing but the mechanics. Ainsley had been in an accident. She'd died. Her baby was with Meg.

He wanted to know more about Ainsley's death. And by the steely resolve in every hard line of his wife's body, she was the one to fill in. She'd been there. She'd been with Ainsley when she passed away.

"Can you get the door?" she said now, her voice softer than before. Gentler. She eased toward him, jarring his attention from her to the suddenly sleeping baby in her arms. "She's out."

His throat burned. Woodenly he stabbed the key into the lock and turned, let Meg breeze by him and into the warm, musty shadows of his sister's home.

And God help him, as she passed it was all he could do not to drown in the scent from so long ago, the one that had once been as familiar to him as the sound of spring rain.

Roses...and baby powder.

EVERYTHING WAS THE SAME. The little living room looked exactly as it had the last time Meg had seen it, two days before Ainsley died.

The wave of grief hit so hard, Meg stopped and bowed her head, took a long deep breath. Let it out slowly.

"You okay?"

She looked up to find Russell lingering in the doorway. Sunlight streaked in from beyond the screened porch. He looked so tall and solid standing there, the lines of his shoulders wide, his jaw square. And for the briefest of moments, it was easy to remember.

"I miss her," she whispered with an honesty that surprised her. But there was no reason to lie. "I was just remembering the last time I was here."

Russell closed the door and with two long strides reached her side. Without being asked, he retrieved an old crocheted afghan and made a pallet on the floor. "Tell me."

Gently, Meg eased Charlotte from her arms to the blanket, holding her steady as she stirred. Did she know? Did she remember, too?

"Ainsley and I were right here," she said, easing back from the sleeping baby. Charlotte's nanny had woken up with a headache, and so Meg had taken over, forcing her to ad-lib her way through the day.

Pushing to her feet, Meg backed away.

Russell matched her step for step.

"With Charlotte." Her throat was thick, tight. "She was on a blanket," she remembered. "Her favorite…a sweet little yellow one. She was up on her hands and her knees, rocking like…"

The warmth of Russell's hand stunned her.

Frozen, she stared at his fingers against her flesh, strong, blunt-tipped—and something inside her stirred.

A touch. It was such a simple thing. People touched every day. Strangers touched. Friends touched. Lovers… touched. The first time Russell had touched her—

She remembered that, the first time. But she did not remember the last.

"Tell me," he said again, and this time she heard it, the soft echo of Scotland. But it didn't caress or seduce, as it once had.

It scraped.

She stepped back, broke the touch. The moment. Didn't want to feel anything. Russell was part of her past.

Charlotte was her future.

Turning, she traded shadows for the bright wash of sunlight in the cheerful yellow kitchen—where a simple little green vase still sat on the round table, next to a big fat paperback. The bookmark was toward the end, waiting for someone to return.

The dead flowers made it clear no one had.

"I can still see her," Meg said as Russell came up behind her. "She was so excited at the thought of Charlotte crawling." And now her baby was about to walk. "She would get down on her hands and knees with her and show her exactly how it was done, and Char would giggle."

A distorted sound broke from Russell, but she did not let herself turn. Did not want to see.

"What happened?"

Meg closed her eyes.

"That night," Russell clarified. "I know there was some kind of accident."

Memories pushed closer. "Don't," she said, turning. She didn't want to go back to that awful place.

But the second she saw the naked, unguarded need in Russell's eyes, she knew she had to. He was Ainsley's brother. He'd loved her. When he'd walked away, it was from Meg, not his sister. She'd simply gotten stuck in the middle.

"It wasn't that late," she said, wishing she'd worn long sleeves. The house had been closed up and the AC wasn't running. She'd expected it to be warm. "Ainsley was coming home from a friend's. Charlotte was in the backseat and—"

Russell's eyes flashed. *"Charlotte was with her?"*

"Sleeping," Meg murmured as she rubbed the chill from her arms. "The State Trooper said it's a miracle she wasn't hurt."

Russell swore under his breath. "I didn't know."

How could he? She'd only talked to his mother that one time.

"It was a drunk driver?" he asked.

She could see the trooper all over again, Ms. Peggy's boy, tall and lanky, shifting from foot to foot. His knock had woken her shortly after midnight. "Yes. He was driving on the wrong side of the highway." At a high rate of speed. "Ainsley swerved and went off the road... hit a tree."

Russell's face darkened. "I should have been here."

Deep inside, a quiet little voice screamed *yes*. *Yes*. He should have been here. For Ainsley...

"It wouldn't have made any difference." The result would have been the same. His sister would still have died.

Russell moved so fast she didn't have time to back away. Look away. He crowded in on her, forcing her to tilt her face to see his. But he did not touch her, not this time.

Not with his hands, anyway.

"You really believe that?"

His voice almost sounded hurt.

Meg swallowed, hard. She wanted to move away, back away. But something deep and powerful held her in place.

"You weren't here," she said quietly. "So I guess we'll never know."

Russell winced. All six foot one of him recoiled, as if she'd taken a willow branch to his bare flesh. He took a step back from her, then stepped back again.

"But *I* was," Meg said, and now her voice broke, and along with it, the dam. "I was here, Russell. I was with her." In the Emergency Room. At the end. "I held her hand," she said through a surge of hot, salty tears. "I held her hand and told her I loved her, that everything would be okay."

Russell looked like he wanted to throw up.

Meg wouldn't let herself back down. "And you know what she said to me?"

His mouth thinned, but he said nothing.

"I can still see her.…" *Hear her.* Massive internal injuries had left Ainsley weak, but not too weak to hold her baby. "In the hospital bed," Meg said, "*with Charlotte…*

"And she asked me," she went on, "she asked me to take care of her baby."

Russell's eyes squeezed shut.

"And you!" The words came out on a broken shout. "She lay there dying, and she asked me to take care of you!"

Slowly Russell's eyes opened, and a tear slipped from the corner.

"You, who walked out on her. You, who left her here, after she'd traveled thousands of miles to be with *you*." Her sainted big brother. "You who *left* her!" she spat, but then remembered the baby and lowered her voice. "You weren't here, Russell. You weren't here when she fell for some young soldier about to deploy for Iraq, when she confused his hunger to live for *love,* when she missed her period.…"

But now he was here, *to settle her affairs.*

It was a little late for that.

"You weren't here…" Meg said again, this time softer.

He hadn't written. Hadn't called. "When Charlotte was born."

When Ainsley died.

But his sister had thought of him anyway. With her final breaths, her final words, she begged Meg to forgive her brother.

"You weren't here." And she didn't want him here now. Didn't want to see him, hear him. Didn't want to feel his hand on her body, his warmth whispering through the coldness.

Biting down on her lip, Meg sucked in a sharp breath and turned, did what Russell had done two years before.

She walked away.

SETTLING SOMEONE'S affairs sounded so tidy and clinical. Like a task to be squeezed into spare time. Come into the house, empty out drawers and cabinets and closets, pack a few boxes. Clear everything out—send it away, throw it away.

But the reality was neither tidy nor clinical. These items weren't just stuff to be sorted and dispensed with; they were the remnants of someone's life. *Ainsley's life.* She'd worn each pair of jeans or shirt or shoes that Meg picked up. She'd loved the pink flip-flops Meg couldn't bring herself to toss, despite the fact they were almost completely worn-out. They'd picked up the satchel purse together at a flea market, along with the ornate cowboy boots. Or rather, boot. The mate was nowhere to be found.

Well over an hour after leaving Russell in the kitchen, Meg secured the top of a box and looked away, toward the simple honey oak dresser. On it sat a perfume bottle, amber in color, delicately curved in shape.

The fragrance was musky, exotic…Ainsley's favorite. For well over the past year, she'd never worn anything else.

Meg crossed to the bottle and picked it up, noticed the writing was in a language she did not recognize. On impulse she lowered her finger and released the scent, inhaled deeply.

For the briefest of seconds, it was as if Ainsley were there.

Knowing that wasn't true, Meg finished clearing the dresser, sorting everything into either the keep, donate or discard box. Somewhere else in the house, Russell worked. Every now and then she heard a bump or a thump, but otherwise they worked in silence.

They were used to that.

The pictures stopped her. In the bottom drawer, tucked away underneath a brightly colored knit scarf, two simple wooden frames lay faceup. In one, two familiar faces greeted Meg. In the other, a complete stranger. And yet, there was something about the sandy-haired young man, the shape of his eyes maybe. *His mouth…*

Meg picked up the frame and removed the picture, turned it over. On the back was a name, a date from a year and a half before…and suddenly Meg realized exactly who she was looking at. The young man with the military-precise haircut and languorous smile— *Tyler,* the name said—was Charlotte's father.

But there was no last name, no town, and there were about a million Tylers in Texas.

Frowning, she placed the photo in the keep box. Someday she would show Charlotte. Someday she would want to know.

The second picture went into the same box, but Meg

did not let herself linger over that one, the snapshot from her honeymoon, taken in the Scottish Highlands.

Without hesitating, she closed the box and pushed it aside, reached for another one. As she worked, she listened for Charlotte, but heard only the soft roll of thunder in the distance.

After stripping the bed, she briskly folded the sheets and old quilt, but could not bring herself to put them in the donate box. Instead she set them aside and went down on her knees, checked the space below.

The boot made her smile. She retrieved it, dragging a flat box out along with it. She was only half paying attention when she lifted the lid—and saw the envelopes. And postcards. Unlike the haphazard way Ainsley lived her life, these were stacked into neat piles. On top of one pile was a picture of some kind, ruins high on a mountaintop. On the other…a pride of lions.

And there in the shadows of Ainsley's bedroom, Meg's heart started to pound so hard she felt it in every pulse point of her body. It echoed in her ears. Because of the envelopes. Airmail. There were no return addresses, but there didn't need to be. The handwriting was enough, the bold masculine scrawl she'd seen hundreds of times before, on notepads, documents… her marriage certificate.

Slowly, methodically, as if she no longer occupied her own body, she lifted the top envelope and dragged her finger along the postmark, felt the room shift.

She knew that date, remembered the week that followed all too well. She'd been here one afternoon, had come over to watch Charlotte while Ainsley ran to the grocery store. Her sister-in-law had been sitting at the kitchen table when Meg arrived—smiling. In her hands, there'd been an envelope.…

But she'd tucked it into a magazine as soon as Meg walked in. A magazine Meg had not seen after Ainsley left.

And now she knew why.

The letter had been from Russell.

Driven by something she didn't understand, Meg picked up the box and turned it upside down, let every letter, every postcard fall to scatter against the old hardwood floor. There, she ran her hand through them, envelope after envelope…image after image. Of South Africa. Egypt. China. Vietnam. Tasmania. Of islands in the South Pacific. Brazil. Peru…

The images blurred…but she knew. She knew why Ainsley had always seemed to know where Russell was.

Because she had.

Blinking, Meg stared down at the jumble of words: *Hi* and *Hello, Miss you* and *Love you, Perfume for you…*

Blanket for Charlotte.

The tears started then, one after another. Her fingers were numb as she reached for the most recent envelope and pulled out the single sheet of loose-leaf paper. She scanned the page line by line, looking for—

She wasn't sure what made her look up. A sound maybe. *A feeling.* Kneeling there beside the small, stripped bed, the letter from Russell to his sister clenched in her fingers, Meg twisted around, and found him. With his shoulder propped against the frame, he dominated the doorway, the dim lighting making the shadow at his jaw look darker. Sterner.

But it was his eyes that drew her, his eyes that made

her breath catch. They were narrow and shuttered, trained exclusively and directly on her.

And in response, something deep, deep inside shifted.

CHAPTER FIVE

Two and a half years before

"WHAT ARE YOU DOING?"

He was angry. She could tell by the way he stood, with his practically nude body dominating the small doorway. The lines of his face were hard. The lines of his body were harder. His chest looked as if were made of stone. His legs looked primed for battle.

He'd been sound asleep when she slipped from bed, the covers tangled down around his hips.

"Couldn't sleep," she said dismissively, refusing to let the accusation in his eyes intimidate her.

"So you're painting?" Once, the remnants of his Scottish ancestry had made his voice supportive. Seductive. Now there were only hard edges, and ridicule. "At three in the morning?"

She ran the roller back against the wall, replacing the warm buttery yellow with the moss-green she'd found in a design magazine. "No time like the—"

"Damn it, Meg." He was across the room in a heartbeat, yanking the roller from her hands. "Stop it."

She stepped back before he could reach for her. "Stop what? Trying to get things done?"

"Pretending," he said, and though his voice was rough from sleep, it didn't carry any warmth. "Stop freaking pretending that this is normal."

And something inside her just...shattered. "You think I'm the one pretending?"

He dropped the roller onto the tarp. "You're damn straight I do. Can you even see yourself, Meg? Do you even know what you're doing? Tearing through the house from one project to another—"

All those broken pieces inside her shifted, sliced at her. But before the pain took control, she shoved it away. "She's gone," she said quietly. "Our little girl is gone, Russell. Nothing can change that."

His eyes went flat. "We can try again."

That's what he always said. "Try what? To replace her?"

"No. Not replace her. We can try for another child—"

He made it sound so sickeningly clinical. Put the past behind them, move on. Try for another child. Forget about the one they lost.

"Not tonight," she said, looking away from him toward the glass of wine on the floor, the wall to the left painted by him, the one to the right by her. "Not tonight."

Present Day

HE KNEW. SHE COULD TELL from the way he looked at her, the knowing etched into the lines of his face. It seemed like a lifetime ago since she'd seen him smile.

He knew what she held in her hand, what she had spread around her. What she'd been doing. And for some crazy reason, Meg felt as if she were sitting there completely naked.

There was no way to deny what she'd been doing. No way to pretend she hadn't been pawing through private words Russell had intended for his sister…and his sister alone.

No way to deny the fact that she'd been wrong.

Not two hours before she'd stood in the kitchen, lashing out at him for abandoning his sister. But the letters and postcards told a far different story.

It stunned her how badly she wanted to pick up each one, read every word.

Words not meant for her.

"I owe you an apology," she surprised herself by saying.

"No, you don't." Unlike the warm, sometimes irreverent thoughts in the letter, these words were blunt, curt. He pushed from the door and crossed the room, closed in on the bed. "You don't owe me anything, Meg."

Meg. It sounded so…cold. "I didn't know you stayed in contact with her."

"There was no reason you should."

For almost two years she'd worked to move forward, stand tall. She'd moved through each day, taught herself not to look back. Sometimes she'd stumbled. Once she'd fallen. But the pieces had come together, until finally she'd reached a point where she no longer felt the stab of vulnerability with every breath she took.

With six little words, Russell brought it all back.

There was no reason you should.

Because the letters were between brother and sister, not man and estranged wife. If he'd wanted her to know what was going on in his life…

If he'd wanted her, he would have written to her.

"I'm glad." She swallowed against the tightness in her throat, realized that she was. No matter what had gone down between Meg and Russell, Ainsley had been an innocent. She had not deserved to lose her brother.

"I'm glad you were there for her," she said, and with the new awareness came a new realization. If Russell had written to Ainsley, then his sister could have written to him. And if she'd written to him...what had she said to him? What had she told him?

How much did he know?

She wanted to search his eyes, to see if they would tell her. But something she didn't understand held her back. Sometimes it was better not to look too hard or too deep, not to ask questions, not unless she really wanted the answer.

She already felt naked enough.

"And I'm glad *you* were there," Russell said, reaching to gather the scattered envelopes back into a pile. "You have no idea how much she idolized you."

Meg's mouth twisted. "*Idolized* is a little strong."

"Her word, not mine," he said, dragging his thumb along Ainsley's name, written in his bold script.

Meg looked away from his ring finger, naked now, not even a hint of a tan line, toward a picture of mist-shrouded Mayan ruins. Machu Picchu, she realized. She and Russell had always talked about going.

He, apparently, had.

"Don't look so stunned," he said, and God help her, there was a warmth to his smile, so unexpected that the coldness seeping through her just...stopped. "You were good for her. You accepted her for who she was, held her hand when no one else would."

Memories washed in, of Ainsley's quirky smile—and the silver rings she wore on every finger.

"But that doesn't mean you have to do this."

She blinked, looked up. "Do what?"

Russell's eyes met hers. "Charlotte."

And somehow Meg knew. Even before he said another word, she knew.

"Taking care of a baby is a lot of work," he went on while she tried to tamp down a quick surge of panic. "Especially one that isn't…"

Just breathing hurt. "Mine?" Once she would have turned away, allowed him to leave the word unspoken. But that was a lifetime ago, when she'd deluded herself into thinking hiding was synonymous with safety. "Is that what you were going to say?"

The hard lines of his face gave away nothing. "She won't always be a sweet little baby who you can cuddle. She'll be a toddler who throws tantrums and a little girl who doesn't always want to do what you do. She'll be a teenager—"

"I'm well aware of that."

"She'll test you, make you crazy. But if this is what you think you want, you have to be there, no matter what. Through thick and thin. You can't just check out because things get rough."

Meg felt her mouth twist, didn't try to stop it. "Wow," she shot back. "To think I thought you knew me."

His eyes met hers. "I thought I did, too."

"Apparently we were both wrong." Anger mixed with the unease. "So let me tell you something, Russell. I couldn't love Charlotte more if she was my flesh and blood. I was there when she was born. I stood up for her when she was baptized. I promised to be there for her, always. And that's what I'm going to do."

For a long moment he said nothing, just looked at her as if she'd become transparent and he could see straight into the deepest, darkest places. Then his gaze softened, and the old Russell was back, the one from all those years before, the one who knew how much love she had in her heart. "Then she's a very lucky little girl."

Meg swallowed. "I'm the lucky one," she whispered.

He held her gaze for a heartbeat longer, then looked away, down toward the postcard still clutched in her fingers.

It was instinct that made her let go, instinct that made her drop the image of Peru before he could reach out—and touch her.

RUSSELL PUT THE LONG, narrow box on the front seat of his rental car, then closed the door and headed for the back porch. He had room for another box or two; everything else would have to wait. The dark clouds to the northwest were pushing closer. It wouldn't be long before the sky opened up.

His thigh throbbed. Pressing his hand to his jeans, he rubbed, but the dull ache persisted. He'd forgotten what it was like to be in Pecan Creek, how thick the air could become in advance of a storm—how discreetly the quiet, tree-lined streets could seep into a man's bones. He'd forgotten how numbing the simplicity could be—how easily the illusion could seduce.

Now, being back…everything blurred all over again, as if he'd walked from stark sunshine into some insidiously dense fog where he couldn't see two feet in front of him.

That's what she'd always done to him.

It was also why he'd left. To breathe, think. To see things clearly.

He kicked an old acorn near the back porch. Christ, when he'd walked into his sister's bedroom to find Meg kneeling there in a soft sweep of filtered sunlight with the postcards scattered around her...

Russell still couldn't figure out what exactly bothered him so much—and that bothered him even more. The look of longing on her face...

It had been years since he'd seen longing of any sort on his wife's face.

And he didn't want it now, not when he knew how badly Meg's make-believe world was about to shatter—and that he was the one who was going to swing the ax. She'd wrapped herself and Charlotte into a cozy little cocoon where all that mattered was the bond they shared. But reality was far more complicated. Meg was not Charlotte's mother. They didn't share blood. But there were those who did, and they were growing restless.

"What happened?"

The quiet voice carried on the wind to swirl through him. He pivoted toward the porch, where he found her standing on the top step. The coming storm lifted the ends of her hair, blowing them against the baby in her arms. Charlotte was awake, but her eyes were heavy as she gazed up at Meg.

Just like when he'd found her earlier, upon his arrival, it was another memory he did not want, an image he'd once looked forward to, coming home to find his wife and daughter greeting him. Over the past two years he'd managed to put all that behind him. Indulging in make-believe wasn't healthy. Their failed marriage had proved that.

But here in Pecan Creek, images of what could have been met him at every turn. His flight next Monday couldn't get here fast enough.

"To your leg?" Meg clarified, her gaze on his thigh, where he still rubbed.

His hand fell away. "It's nothing."

"You're limping."

"Just the rain," he said, glancing toward the clouds. "The barometric pressure."

"Barometric pressure," she repeated. "Just like that, you're suddenly a human barometer?"

The quick spurt of laughter surprised him—who was this woman? Only seconds before, everything inside him had been twisted like barbed wire, but the way she stood there on the back porch with the baby propped on her hip...

He might as well have been a ten-year-old trying to explain how the big picture window got broken.

"Apparently," he agreed, closing the gap between them. With effort, he kept his strides even. "Can come in pretty handy, too—"

"Russell."

The familiarity in her voice—*the awareness in her eyes*—killed the fun and games. Little Charlotte babbled away, once again pawing at Meg's chest. But Meg wasn't smiling as she usually did when she held Charlotte. She almost looked stricken.

"Tell me," she said, and this time her voice was quiet. Firmer. "What happened to your leg? Were you in an accident?"

He reached the bottom step as a raindrop splashed on his arm. "It was a long time ago."

She stepped back from the splatter of the storm. "Not that long ago," she said quietly. "You've only been gone..." She looked away, toward the gnarled branches of the old post oaks.

Twenty-two months. He'd been gone twenty-two months.

It might as well have been twenty-two years. They'd both been broken back then, in heart, in spirit. He was broken in body now, but she…

She was radiant.

And it slayed him. It slayed him how beautiful she looked standing with her shoulder-length hair blowing against her face, the soft light in eyes that had been dull and flat when he left, the fullness to a face that had been tired and gaunt, the strength in her clearly supple body…the baby in her arms.

Their little girl would have been two years old now.

He thought about that sometimes, dreamed about her when he fell too deeply asleep. He could see her there in the shadows, a smiling little girl with her mother's eyes.

He ripped his gaze away from Meg and Charlotte, looking instead toward the small empty house where his sister had lived.

"It was in Africa, about a month after I got there."

That had been his first assignment, the reason he'd walked out the door that night a lifetime before. Just a quick assignment, four weeks, six at the most. Go to Mozambique, document the civil uprising, return to Pecan Creek. He'd never intended to stay away.

"It started as a cut," he muttered as Meg looked back toward him, and then it was slow motion all over again, the juxtaposition between his wife and the baby, the simplicity of a warm spring day in Texas versus the unmitigated hell he'd walked into. "I was at a field hospital," he said. "They were understaffed."

Meg's expression tensed. "As a patient?"

"Volunteering." Before Meg, he'd been able to separate work from life. But there in Africa, with his own life so twisted up, there'd been no way to stand there with his freaking camera and just…take pictures. Not when mothers cried and children lay dying. "I—I…" He wanted to look away from her, but something inside fed on the warmth in her eyes. The compassion.

There'd been no compassion before, when he'd needed—

His wife.

"A nurse was running," he said. "She tripped—I tried to catch her—" But they'd both gone down. "Instead I caught her scalpel in my thigh."

Meg frowned. "Ouch."

"It wasn't too deep," he said, but his hand went to his leg anyway, and rubbed. "Just a puncture wound mostly."

Meg spider-crawled her fingers along Charlotte's chest, earning full baby belly laughs. But she never took her eyes from Russell. "But in Mozambique…"

"Infection set in." It had been bad. For a while, they'd insisted he would need to lose his leg. "If I'd stayed—" He broke off when her eyes went dark.

"You went home—" she started, then corrected herself. "To Scotland."

He knew the exact second she put the pieces together. Her body straightened. The soft line of her mouth hardened. But it was her eyes that got him, the dull, vacant glaze that threw him back in time. "To a hospital in Edinburgh."

She slid her hand around Charlotte, pulling the baby closer. "That's why Ainsley went back. To see you."

He hated the betrayal in her gaze. It was one thing

for her to resent him. But his sister was no longer here to defend herself.

"She never said a word," Meg whispered.

And he could tell how badly that reality stung. She didn't like being left out of decisions. "Meg, I'm sorry."

"Did you ask her not to?"

Memories rolled over him, hazy, dark like the clouds closing in on Pecan Creek. There'd been a fever. He'd hallucinated. He'd grabbed her hand and held on, asked her to never leave.

But when he opened his eyes, it had been Ainsley sitting by his bed. Ainsley quietly crying.

"We weren't together," he said. And they hadn't been for a long time.

"No," Meg said, but there was no emotion in her voice. No tears in her eyes. "We weren't."

The ache in his thigh radiated in all directions. "I—I…" Christ, he did not need this. But like removing a bandage, he knew the slower he moved, the worse it would get. "I got the papers your lawyer sent," he said. Her call about Ainsley had not gotten through, but the divorce papers had. "I brought them with me."

She just stood there. The wind kept blowing, Charlotte kept fiddling with everything she could get her curious little hands on, but Meg, Christ, she just stood there.

She just freaking stood there.

They might as well have been discussing the weather.

And that cold, polite indifference fired through him

with an intensity that made him want to destroy the distance between them, take her in his arms and—

And.

It was always the "and" that got him.

CHAPTER SIX

Two years before

"I PICKED UP SOME WINE on the way home, a cab."

On the other side of the small room she used as an office, Meg kept tapping at the keys of her laptop.

"I poured you some," Russell said, moving into the room. He hated how tentative he felt, like a stranger in his own home. "Here." He extended one of the crystal goblets they'd received as wedding presents. She'd been so excited....

"In a minute." She never looked up.

Glancing over her shoulder, he saw the editorial raising questions about the new research institute going in west of town. "It's your favorite," he said. "From that little winery—"

Her fingers stilled against the keys. "Russell." Her eyes flashed as she looked up. "I said in a minute."

And something inside him...snapped. She always said "just a minute." "Not now." "Maybe later." "Tomorrow."

"I heard you." It was all he could do to set the glass down gently, rather than slam it against the hardwood of the bookshelf. "Just like I heard you last night and last week..." He stepped toward her, saw her wince. "Damn it, Meg!"

Thoughts blurred. Control shattered. He reached for

her even as she jerked back, took her arms and pulled her to her feet. "Do you hear yourself?" he asked. "Do you know how long it's been?"

Everything about her froze. His wife...froze. "You're not really going back to that again, are you?"

"Back. To. That." The words tore out of him. "Is that what making love is to you now...that?"

She made it sound like something dirty and dreaded.

Eyes that had once been vibrant and blue went dark as she looked up at him. "Russell, please."

"Please...what?" She was still in his arms. His hands were still on her body. Her face was inches away. "Go away? Leave you alone?" Nothing. No change in her expression. No denial. "Never come back?"

Now she moved. Now she looked down. "Please don't do this."

Something dark and desperate shifted through him. This was his wife. This woman, this stranger...was his wife. Once she'd promised to have and to hold, in good times and bad...

Now she couldn't even look at him.

"Meggie." He hated the way his voice thickened on her name. He was on his knees, goddamn it, on his freaking knees. "I don't want to do this alone."

Her eyes lifted, and for the briefest of seconds he saw her, *his wife*. And that was all it took for him to pull her closer and bring his mouth to hers, to crush her against him and drink—

She twisted away with a violence that left him standing there, stripped to the bone.

Hand against her mouth, as if rubbing away something ugly and filthy, she turned and hurried from the room.

He did not follow.

Present Day

CHARLOTTE SLEPT. Meg eased the baby from her arms to her crib and gently pulled up the soft chenille blanket. After raising the rail, she turned and slipped from the room. Sometimes, just the crack of her ankles was all it took to wake Charlotte up.

Door closed, she made her way to her office and fired up her laptop, glanced at Julia's proposal for an allegedly explosive exposé before pulling up the outline for the festival. With only two days left, it was time to double- and triple-check every last detail.

Russell had the papers. He was ready to sign. Just a technicality, really. Their marriage had been over for years.

But that didn't stop the slow, steady leak inside her, the coldness oozing into places she'd thought permanently walled off. A simple signature shouldn't make any difference. She was the one who'd initiated the divorce. She was the one who'd had the papers drawn up.

She just hadn't expected him to come home to sign them.

Seeing him again…

No, she told herself. No. She wasn't going to do that, wasn't going to dwell on the situation or torture herself. Russell's eyes didn't matter. Nor did the minefield of memories she'd tiptoed through that afternoon at Ainsley's house.

But the restlessness lingered, no matter how many times she read the same bullet points detailing the silent auction. Giving up, she headed for a shower, but wound up in the kitchen instead. Robotically, she retrieved the five-year-old cab from the cabinet above the oven. In the drawer by the stove she found the corkscrew. From the china cabinet…a single crystal goblet.

And from somewhere long, long ago, the memory stirred…

It's your favorite…from that little winery—

She'd never let him finish. She'd looked at him standing there with that glass of wine in his hands and the hunger in his eyes…and she'd known. She'd known what he wanted, and it hadn't been to give her a glass of wine. At least, not because he wanted her to relax.

He'd wanted what he'd always wanted…her.

He'd wanted to go back in time, to pretend. He'd wanted things to be simple, uncomplicated. Easy. He'd wanted her to be someone she no longer was.

She'd wanted to scream.

When he'd touched her, when he'd pulled her into his arms and slanted his mouth against hers, she thought she had.

But maybe it had only been inside.

She'd done that a lot back then, screamed at the top of her lungs. But no one had heard. The wine had helped. At first.

Then Russell had left. She'd thought the screaming would stop then. And during the bright hours of the day, when she'd been busy and absorbed by the *Gazette,* it had. But when she'd come home, the screaming had started all over again, sharp and stabbing and silent, over and over. There'd only been one way to make it stop.

One way to make everything stop.

Craving that same numbness, she looked at the smoky bottle sitting beside Charlotte's pink sippy cup…and her hands started to shake. She lifted the corkscrew anyway and wedged open the bottle, inhaled deeply. Closed her eyes as the once-familiar musky scent drifted through her. Just one glass. Just to help her relax.

Just. One.

Just. Tonight.

Without thinking, she picked up the bottle and tilted it toward the glass, poured, watched the deep burgundy liquid slosh up against the crystal edges before sliding back down to settle in the bottom.

Meg picked up the glass and drew it to her mouth. Closed her eyes. Inhaled deeply. Soon Ainsley's affairs would be settled and Russell would be gone. It was what she wanted. She'd be able to breathe then.

She'd be able to forget about dreams that had died so very long ago.

NIGHT FELL SOFTLY in Pecan Creek. The brunt of the storm had skirted south of town, providing a lightning show but little else. Now high, thin clouds skittered across an almost-full spring moon. The air was slow, thick— drenched with the perfume of azaleas and dogwood and the lilacs dripping from vines twined along an old fence.

Russell couldn't sleep. That happened a lot. Doctors had prescribed medication. A New Age friend had offered up hypnosis and ambient music. But rarely did Russell sleep more than three hours at a stretch, five hours combined. Instead, he walked.

There was something calming about being awake when everyone else slept, something grounding about walking a deserted street. Sometimes he brought his camera. A cat, an owl, a flower against the darkness… he never knew what would catch him.

But tonight he walked alone.

He'd always been a wanderer. A nomad. He'd left

Scotland at eighteen, craving…something. Something more. Adventure. Restlessness had driven him, a hunger to do and see and experience. Until Meg. Then he'd just wanted Meg.

He'd traveled the world over. He'd seen beauty and glamour, architectural marvels and untold luxury, the kind that only ridiculous amounts of money could buy. Never would he have imagined that something as simple and benign as springtime in a small Texas town would finally let him exhale.

The tree-lined streets had a grace to them, all the tired, sleeping houses. Many of them had stood for over a century—the stone house he'd grown up in had stood for over two. Maybe that's why he'd always been drawn to Pecan Creek's historic district. It was about as old as you could get in a country younger than his hometown.

He still remembered Meg's face the first time she'd seen the run-down old house: it had not been love at first sight. He'd seen the potential, but it had taken time for Meg to see the promise behind overgrown vegetation and years of disrepair.

Russell slowed as headlights swept in from behind him. The sound of a car engine grew louder, until finally the squad car emerged beside him—and pulled over. A second later a slightly tinted window lowered to reveal the wary-eyed driver.

"Evenin', sir," the young man said.

Twenty-five, Russell guessed. Thirty tops. "Evenin'," he said back.

"Something I can help you with?"

Time rolled forward, Russell knew. Only two years before Pecan Creek had been his home. Now this young deputy watched him with suspicious eyes, as if he was a potential axe murderer, or worse.

"Just taking a walk," he answered. Granted, it was getting close to midnight and almost everyone else in town slept.

The deputy shifted the cruiser into Park and leaned toward the window. "Got some ID on you?"

Russell wasn't sure what he wanted more—to swear under his breath...or sigh. "Sure do," he said, reaching to slide his license from his wallet. It would expire in six months. He'd have to replace it then, trade his Texas driver's license for that of Scotland or wherever home became.

The deputy took the small card and, with a big Maglite, looked it over. Slowly, his eyes lifted back to Russell. "You're Meg's ex."

Russell felt a muscle twitch in the hollow of his cheek. "Not yet."

"I remember you," the deputy said as he glanced in his rearview mirror. "Didn't hear you were back in town." His attention returned to Russell. "Can I give you a ride somewhere?"

"I'm good."

But the deputy didn't want to let go of his bone. "Where are you staying?"

"At the Manor."

"Sir, that place has been closed for over a year."

So it had. "Liz is a friend of mine." He'd always had a soft spot for the owner's granddaughter during her internship at the *Gazette,* despite the way she'd always wanted to embellish the simplest of facts. "She's letting me stay as a trial run."

The deputy frowned. "You know I'll need to check that out," he said.

And now Russell did know what he wanted to do—and it wasn't sigh. "Go right ahead," he invited, retrieving his license and returning it to his wallet. The back-and-forth went on for another minute or so before the deputy finally drove off.

Russell watched the taillights disappear down the street, in the direction of the historic district. Poor Liz. He hoped she wasn't asleep. He started to follow, but hesitated. Ten minutes to the right would take him back to town, to the Magnolia Manor where the deputy was no doubt heading. But just a minute to the left was the house that had once been home. Straight to the cemetery where they'd buried their little girl, whom they'd lost before she'd even drawn a breath.

He was a man of motion. He was constantly on the go, moving. Stillness was not in his nature. When something fell, he picked it up. When a question arose, he found an answer. When adventure called, he went after it. When something broke, he fixed it.

He'd not been able to fix Meg.

She hadn't wanted him to.

He hated how badly the reality of that burned. She'd been his wife. He'd loved her with a passion he'd never before known. But after they'd lost Hope, the woman he'd loved, the woman he'd thought he'd known, had simply…gone away. She'd shut him out with airtight precision.

But now she smiled again. Now she laughed. She thrived. Because of Charlotte. Ainsley had told him that, how amazing his wife and niece were together. And here, now, he could see it for himself.

But no blood bound them together—and his parents were making noises about wanting to know their grandchild. With less than a week left in town, Russell knew he had to tell Meg. He'd been about to that afternoon, but then he'd seen the devotion in Meg's eyes—a happiness that had not been there for far too long—and the words had gone away.

From the corner where he stood he could see the house farther down the street, across from the parked car, the dogwood in bloom. A single light glowed from the window at the far end of the porch. The nursery. She would be in there, with the baby.

It was a sight he'd craved for the better part of the past ten years.

Slowly he turned. His thigh ached. He slid his hand to massage it, even as his thoughts slid to another time. Once, in what seemed like another life, she'd run her hands all over his body....

His pace picked up. Another car drove by. Soon he would be back at the Manor.

With luck, the ghosts would stay away.

"SORRY I'M LATE!"

With the afternoon sun slanting in from a wall of windows, Lori and Julia twisted toward the door to the conference room.

"No worries," Lori said as Meg breezed in and dropped her overflowing briefcase into one of the empty chairs. "Everything set?"

Setting down a huge foam cup, Meg riffled through the press of folders. "With a wing and a prayer," she said.

"Please." That was Julia, of course. "Since when do you leave anything to prayer?"

"Editorial" file in hand, Meg glanced at her cousin and smiled. She'd been on the go since seven in the morning, with back-to-back meetings and a quick smoothie for a late lunch as she'd walked from the library back to the *Gazette*. She was lucky to have such a great staff at the paper.

"Where are we?" she asked, reaching for a tablet of paper and her favorite purple pen.

Julia tapped her finger against the yellow notepad in front of her. "Circulation down another two percent," she said. Then, "People seriously need to quit dying in this town."

Meg grinned. "Then there would be no obits," she said, with one last sip of her strawberry-banana smoothie. "And we'd lose the other half of our subscribers."

It was an age-old joke. Nothing kept a paper going like death. Except over the past several years, as Pecan Creek's elderly passed on, so did subscriptions. Twenty- and thirtysomethings had little interest in a physical newspaper. Before he left town, Russell had been spearheading a more interactive online experience.

Glancing at Lori, Meg noticed how tired her friend looked, her face about two shades too pale. "Everything okay, hon?"

Lori nodded, but the worry in her eyes deepened.

Meg was pretty sure it had nothing to do with the *Gazette*'s subscription problems. But until Lori was ready to talk, there was little Meg could do, other than offer support.

"What about the Web site?" Lori had suggested a monthly contest. "Are hits still climbing?"

She nodded. "Up five percent over last month," she said, sliding a sheet of paper across the table.

"Very good."

"Did you get a chance to read my proposal?" Julia asked as Meg glanced at Lori's detailed Web activity report. She didn't really want to have this conversation again.

Julia was bored. The day-to-day chore of running the paper did little to fulfill her need to get her hands dirty. She had hardly any formal journalism training, but that didn't stop her from fancying herself the next *60 Minutes* superstar. While Lori worked steadily at growing the *Gazette*'s Web presence, Julia insisted the only way to maintain the viability of the paper was to come up with new content, the more riveting, more controversial, the better.

Not an easy task for a small East Texas town where big news consisted of a brawl at the city council meeting or ghosts at the local bed-and-breakfast.

"I did," Meg said, meeting Julia's bulldog-determined gaze head-on. She'd been up deep into the hours of early morning, first with a restless baby, then with a series of reports and proposals pertaining to the newspaper.

"What do you think?" Julia asked, referring to her plan to infiltrate the new research institute just east of town. She was convinced there was something odd going on.

Meg tended to think her cousin had been reading too many thrillers.

"It's perfect, isn't it?" Julia's eyes literally glowed. "When do you want me to start?"

Meg chose her words carefully. "Jules. I appreciate your enthusiasm—"

"Then let me do it," she pressed before Meg could finish. "This is exactly the kind of boost the paper needs—I'd bet my last dollar there's more going on at Brookhaven than sleep research. I've been reading about the director all over the Internet—did you know Noah Blackstone used to be CIA?"

That was news to Meg. "What about Lance?" she asked, intrigued despite her better judgment. "Are he and Austin on board?"

Julia's face froze—and Meg had her answer. "They will be."

In other words, Julia hadn't mentioned her big plan to go undercover by posing as a patient to her husband or son yet.

"Look, I'm all for trying something new," Meg said carefully. "I'm just not sure now is the right time."

Julia went very still. They'd known each other all their lives, but that didn't mean she played patty-cake. "What are you afraid of, Meg? You know good and well if Russell were still managing editorial, he'd be all over it."

Everything inside Meg tightened. It was a low blow and they all knew it. "Well, he's not, is he? And even if he was—"

"Oh!" Lori suddenly said, leaning forward to allow a sweep of jet-black hair to swing against her cheek. "Speaking of Russ, did you know he was coming here today?"

Meg sat back. "Here?"

"Just after lunch," Lori said. "He said he wanted to see his old office."

Instinct had Meg glancing left, to the wall the conference room shared with the storage room, which had once been Russell's office.

"Don't worry," Julia put in, and her voice was a little more wry, not quite as combative. "We told him where to go."

The smile just kind of happened, and with it, the tension of moments before lessened. "I bet you did."

"You're so bad," Lori said, finally looking a little less serious. Then she added, "Oh! Rosemary called…"

CLOUDS GATHERED on the horizon. They were darker than the day before, angrier. Typical of April, there was a stillness to the early-evening air Meg automatically recognized, the drop in barometric pressure that always preceded spring storms. When unstable air moved east across Texas, Mother Nature put on a show.

Through the premature darkness Meg hurried to the back porch, readying her apology for Charlotte's nanny. She'd tried to call Rosemary back, but both cell phone and home phone had rolled to voice mail. They'd probably been in the bathroom, Meg figured. Or out for a walk or at the grocery store.

The breeze whipped at the branches of the old post oaks scattered about the backyard as Meg slid her key into the door. She pushed inside the utility room and started to call out, but stilled when she noticed the quiet. And the darkness. Silently she checked her watch, saw that it was closing in on seven.

Careful not to make a noise, she slipped into the kitchen and deposited her briefcase and purse on the table, kicked off her sandals. She'd take over from Rosemary and make sure all was settled, then think about dinner. She was pretty sure she still had some salmon in the fridge.

With luck, the coming storm wouldn't wake the baby.

The memory hit with the low rumble of thunder in the distance. For two years she'd been like Teflon, never allowing anything unwanted to penetrate her hard shell. But as she stood barefoot in the shadows of early evening with a storm rolling in from the west, the images played like a faded slide show through her mind. The rain, the wind. Vibrant streaks of cloud-to-ground lightning dancing across the sky. The candles and battery-operated radio. The old blanket and two pillows on the floor of the patio. And him.

Russell.

Meg closed her eyes, but the memory lingered. They'd loved storms, had often gone out on the porch to watch the clouds tumble in. There was nothing like making love while the world trembled.

She opened her eyes and stared into the darkness. But no matter how hard she tried, she could not remember the last time she'd *remembered*. The last time there'd been anything but…regret. Their final months together, during the dark empty days after they lost their baby, they'd been strangers living in familiar bodies. They'd forgotten how to touch. How to talk.

How to love.

But now…

Now nothing, she told herself. Once she'd thought she'd love him forever—and there was no denying that he was a very attractive man. Even the limp served to *add,* rather than take away. There was a gravity to him that had not been there before, an awareness in the dark green of his eyes. It was only natural that she would remember.

Just as it was only natural that once he left—*again*—she would forget. Again.

With the howl of the wind against the windows growing louder, she slipped from the kitchen to find Rosemary—and saw him.

CHAPTER SEVEN

Two years before

QUIET ECHOED THROUGH the house. That was the first
thing Meg noticed when she opened the back door. She
knew Russell was home—she'd seen his SUV in the
garage. The absolute silence was odd.

Inside, she put her briefcase and purse on the old
farmhouse table and headed into the kitchen. After the
day she'd had at the paper, she needed a glass of wine
to help her unwind.

The duffel bag stopped her. Stuffed full, it sat by
the table along with the backpack Russell used as a
briefcase. They went with him everywhere, had been
in more countries than she had been in states. He'd had
them with him when he arrived in Pecan Creek all those
years before, standing in the doorway to her office with
one slung over his shoulder, one at his feet.

"Good, you're here."

She looked up to see him emerge from the family
room. He was fully dressed, not in sweats and socks as
he usually was in the evening, but in his favorite wool
blend sweater, the burnt orange one that made his eyes
look like emeralds. His favorite low-slung jeans…his
favorite loafers.

"I—I…" He stopped a few feet from her, hesitating.

Russell Montgomery never hesitated.

"I was hoping…you'd be home in time," he said, and the vague unease she'd sensed blossomed into something much closer to panic.

"Home…for what?" she asked.

He glanced at his duffel bag for what seemed like an eternity before looking back at her. "Lucas called. They're doing a documentary on Mozambique—"

"You're leaving." The words—the freezing realization—scraped on the way out. The truth stung.

"Just for a few weeks."

Somewhere inside, she started to shake. She looked at him standing there, her husband, the father of her little girl, a stranger in the kitchen where they'd once made love. It had all been so easy then. They'd laughed. They'd shared.

Now every time he touched her, inside she screamed.

"I'll be back," he said.

But Meg did not move. She didn't know how to. She didn't trust herself to. If she moved she might run to him. And if she ran to him, she might fall apart.

So she stood in the dim lighting of the kitchen and pressed her lips together, nodded. "Okay."

His eyes flashed with something wild and dark. It was the only warning she got. Before she could so much as draw a breath he reached for her, dragging her across the distance between them and crushing her in his arms, his mouth moving over hers, hard and hungry, seeking…demanding.

But Meg just stood there. She wanted—

God, she wanted so bad.

But she didn't know what.

To feel…something. Anything.

To breathe.

With a harsh sound Russell pulled back and stared down at her, the storm in his eyes ripping through her with shattering violence.

Then he stepped back. "I—I'll…call you."

She swallowed. Nodded. "Okay."

And then he walked out the door.

At the front window she watched his taillights fade into nothingness. Then and only then did she close her eyes—and breathe.

Present Day

HE LAY AGAINST THE RICH brown of the sofa, his back propped against the wide curved arm, an old quilt covering his lower body. His face was relaxed, his eyes closed. Like his feet, his chest was bare, save for the baby sprawled on top.

Outside the big picture window, the post oaks kept dancing, but inside the quiet house, Meg went completely still.

Through the shadows she stared at them, Russell and Charlotte, uncle and niece, but saw only a flash of the past, a sharp glimmer of a future that had never come to be. He'd so wanted to be a father.

Her chest locked up. Her throat tightened. Numbly she lifted a hand to find her heart…and rubbed. The thrum was hard and erratic, and even as Meg drank in the sight, it hurt.

She wasn't sure how long she stood there. Maybe a few minutes. Maybe longer. They looked so peaceful, man and child, both with their eyes closed, their breath rising and falling in unison. Charlotte had her little arms sprawled against her uncle, her chubby hand resting against a scattering of wiry chest hair. Once dark, now sprinkled with gray. Russell's arms were around the baby, one hand against the top of her back, the other over her legs, so protective, as if he never meant to let her go.

Somehow Meg ripped herself away. Somehow she made herself return to the kitchen. She stood at the sink with her hands beneath the running water, looking beyond the carefully tended African violets, through the window toward the clouds. It wouldn't be much longer before the storm hit.

The irony made her laugh out loud.

"Meg."

She stiffened, the warm cadence of his voice washing over her. Lifting her eyes to the window, transformed by the darkness into a mirror, she found him lounging in the doorway behind her. As always he looked tall, hard. Except for the yellow blanket slung around his hips. That was soft. She was pretty sure the rest of him was...

Naked, she realized.

Just as he had so many times before, Russell Montgomery was standing in her kitchen, naked.

Words failed her. She scrambled around for something intelligent to say—or witty, pithy, sarcastic even—but the sight of her soon-to-be ex-husband standing a few feet behind her, naked save for the chenille baby blanket around his hips, pretty much stripped away everything else. For a heartbeat the years and hurt between them fell away, leaving just the two of them standing in familiar territory—the kitchen, as they had countless times before.

She'd forgotten. So much. She'd forgotten how comfortable he'd always been in his body, the way the gleam in his eyes could cut straight through her, the purely kinetic way her body responded...to his. It had been like that from the start, when she'd been twenty-three years old and he'd strolled into the lecture hall as if he owned the place. There'd been over two hundred students present, but from the second her eyes had met his, there'd been no one but him.

Just like now.

He'd always been able to do that, make everyone else—*everything else*—simply fade away.

Except in the end. In the end, when it mattered most, the magic between them had failed.

"You always had a knack for making an entrance," she managed to say, but it was the exits that sent a forgotten ache splintering through her.

His mouth twitched into a lopsided smile. "Didn't mean to startle you."

She didn't want to laugh. She didn't. But the megamajor understatement had her twisting toward him, her brows shooting up. "Oh...okay," she said. "I guess you thought it would be perfectly normal to come up behind me wearing only—" she flicked her gaze down to the fluffy yellow blanket "—well, I'd have to call it a loincloth."

She didn't want him to laugh, either. She didn't want to hear that masculine shout from low in his throat. She didn't want the rich sounds to mix with the thunder and fill the normally quiet kitchen.

But the hard, controlled mask of his face softened into familiar lines—and he laughed. "Well, there you go."

And she smiled. For that moment, it was all so warm and easy. "Yellow always was your color."

He shifted, striking a goofy male model pose. "It's not like I had much choice."

"Riiiiight." Grinning, she crossed to him and lifted a hand to swat at him, the way she'd done so many times before. But the moment before contact she froze, the imaginary force field sliding efficiently into place.

He must have felt it, too, because with the same swiftness the teasing faded from his eyes and he straightened. "I stopped by to check on Charlotte—"

"You stopped by?" There was an edge to her voice she didn't understand, a skitter of panic low in her stomach. He was Charlotte's uncle, Ainsley's brother. They shared more than just impossibly green eyes. They shared blood. If he decided to fight Meg for custody, it was hard to imagine a judge siding in her favor.

"I—I…" He frowned. "I thought it would be better if you weren't around."

Somehow she didn't wince. But she could do nothing about the quick stab of cold.

His eyes darkened. It was almost as if…he knew. And felt it, too.

"I didn't want to upset you," he said, and his voice was quieter, less sure. "I thought—"

"Don't." The word came out harsher than she intended, but she made no move to soften it. She didn't want that from him. She didn't want him worrying about her.

"She's your niece," she said. "You're welcome to see her anytime you wish." Briskly, she stepped back and openly appraised him. "But in the future, it might be better if you brought your own blanket."

His mouth quirked into the faintest ghost of a smile. "I'll remember that."

"A little bigger," she said before she realized how the words might sound.

His eyes took on a forgotten gleam, but before he could say anything, Meg pressed on.

"Rosemary went home?" she asked.

Russell held her gaze a heartbeat longer than necessary before answering. A good two feet separated them, but when he looked at her like that…warm…familiar… he didn't need his body to touch her.

"She wasn't feeling well," he finally said. "Had a headache, wanted to get some rest."

Meg frowned. "That must have been why she called earlier."

"It was," Russell said. "Charlotte was a little fussy, too, and Rosemary was hoping you could get home—"

Meg didn't let him finish. She slipped by him and hurried into the family room, where the baby lay sprawled on the big overstuffed sofa, secured by a cocoon of cushions and throw pillows.

"She's fine now," Russell whispered. He came up behind her, so close the warmth of his breath whispered against Meg's neck. "I gave her a bottle—"

Meg twisted around. "She threw up." That's why Russell was undressed.

He nodded. "She did."

"I'm sorry."

His eyes sparkled. "No worries."

At six-two, he was a good eight inches taller than Meg, bringing her eyes level with his pecs. He'd always taken good care of himself—running, push-ups, sit-ups—and through the shadows of the storm, she could see that in that regard, little had changed since she'd last lifted her hand to his chest. She'd loved to touch him there, to tease first with her fingers, then her mouth—

Abruptly she looked up. "Your clothes—"

"In the dryer."

They stood beside a sleeping baby...a baby who'd thrown up all over him. They hadn't seen each other in two years, not since he'd taken a four-week assignment and never come home. It was ridiculous the way her body hummed.

So long, she knew. It had been so long since she'd let herself feel anything. Since she'd let herself touch, or be touched. Since she'd...wanted. Anything. Once she'd known this man with soul-blistering intimacy. It was only natural that standing here now, like this, would resurrect—

"I couldn't find any clothes." His words were as naked as he was, and with them the past two years slid quickly and soberly back into place.

Mouth dry, she stepped back. God, had she really been about to go up on her toes and touch him? "In the attic," she said.

He looked down at her, watching her carefully, almost as if he expected her to vanish if he so much as blinked. "I figured you must have given them away."

She almost had. When four weeks had stretched into eight, eight into six months. When she'd realized that "see you later" had really been goodbye.

"Not my place," she answered with an honesty that surprised her. "They weren't mine to give."

She would have sworn he winced. "You could have," he said quietly. "I would have understood. I didn't need them...."

Anymore.

The wind whipped through the trees, the sky flashing

with increasing frequency. "You know me," she said, trying to lighten things up. "I've never been very good at—"

Letting go.

She'd never been very good at letting go.

There wasn't much distance between them, a foot, maybe two. It was Russell who moved first. At least she thought it was. He stepped toward her, forcing her to tilt her face to see him. In some vague, barely functioning corner of her mind she saw him lift a hand. Felt the warmth slide against her face. She was moving then, toward him, pushing up on her toes with a longing that seeped through her like water from a ground spring.

"Meggie," he murmured, and then she wasn't thinking anymore. Was only feeling. And remembering.

Wanting.

His mouth came down softly, whispering against hers with a tenderness that ripped at her, a sadness she instinctively wanted to chase away. Lifting her arms seemed the most natural thing in the world. Putting her hands to the hard, hot curve of his shoulder, sliding them around to his back. Slanting her mouth against his. Gentle at first. Tentative. Exploring.

Longing.

Lightning danced and thunder applauded, while memories washed and clashed and fed, opening her to him, offering even as she took. She heard the low, guttural sound, but didn't know whose throat it ripped from. She only knew that his arms were around her and hers around him, her hand fisted in his dark copper hair, that their bodies were pressed together, were one, that his whiskers scraped her face as she greedily took—

She didn't know what stopped her. The storm still

seduced, even as the baby slept. Russell still held on, his eyes glazed and heavy and…hungry.

But everything inside Meg went stone-cold. She stood there frozen in his arms, acutely aware of every hard line and bulge of his body.

And the warmth and aching within hers.

"I'm sorry." And she was. So very horribly sorry. For everything.

Maybe she spoke aloud. Maybe the words were nothing but a silent scream. It didn't matter. Numbly she twisted from him and hurried toward the darkness of the hallway, away. That was all she could think.

Away.

HE FOUND HER IN THE ATTIC.

Almost twenty minutes had passed since she'd ripped from his arms and run from him. Run. From him. *Her husband.* He'd stood there a long while, staring after her, waiting—

Wanting.

Christ, the wanting was the worst. After all this time, he knew she wasn't coming back. That what he wanted most didn't even exist anymore. It had died with their little girl. But the wanting lingered, like some bizarre masochistic residue, long after everything else finally let go. Every time his cell phone rang. Every time a text message arrived. Sometimes he'd spin around for no apparent reason.

Now from the top of the pull-down stairs, he watched her kneeling toward the back of the attic. There was only one light, an overhead lantern several feet from the entrance, casting a veil of light and shadow out in all directions. She knelt beside a big plastic tub, baby clothes neatly folded in her lap.

Little girl clothes, with the tags still attached.

All that sexual zing he'd felt following the surprise kiss evaporated into complete hollowness. Coming back to Pecan Creek had seemed so simple, clinical even. He'd come, take care of business, leave.

But this time he would not leave alone.

Quietly, he moved through the maze of boxes and crates, waiting until he was only a few feet away before speaking. He didn't want to raise his voice, not here, surrounded by relics of a life that never had a chance to live.

"You kept everything."

He saw her stiffen, saw her hands tighten against the sweet little pink booties he'd secretly had made. For a long moment she didn't move, just knelt with her head bowed, as if in prayer. Then she looked up—and damn near destroyed him with her dark, damp eyes.

She was crying. His Meg—Meg the Strong, Meg the Brave—was crying.

"Meggie," he said, going down on his knee and reaching for her. But he stopped when he saw her wince, knew that she did not want him to touch her.

She looked fragile. There was no other word for it. She was a woman who prided herself on putting on a tough face, on holding herself together and trudging forward, no matter how stark the adversity. Even when her mother had developed stage-two breast cancer. Meg had only been twenty-four at the time, going to school in New York. But from the moment she'd received the phone call from Texas, nothing else had mattered. She'd shuttered away her dreams and packed up her bags, saying goodbye and returning to Pecan Creek without voicing a single regret. He'd been haunted by that during the long months he'd spent in the Middle

East, consumed by the need to make it better for her. Somehow.

And then, after Hope…God, she'd gone into absolute complete and total lockdown, shutting him out. Shutting everyone out. He'd recognized it at the time, he'd held on and he'd fought, slamming into brick wall after brick wall, until finally he'd become numb to it all.

Now he looked at her kneeling in the shadows of the attic, holding the booties their daughter never had a chance to wear. Tears slid down her face.

The urge to wipe them away was as basic, as intrinsic, as breathing.

"I was looking for your clothes," she said quietly, with the faintest of smiles. Blond hair fell against her face, tangled now, scraggly. But beautiful all the same. "They're in that box there," she said, gesturing toward a big blue plastic tub.

But he didn't need them anymore. The dryer had finished. His own jeans and T-shirt were clean now, back on his body. "Thanks."

"You can take them with you," she said. "I don't need—" She broke off, lifted her eyes to his.

She didn't need them anymore.

"I probably don't, either," he started, then rocked back on his heels. "Unless that New Orleans T-shirt is in there."

Her smile widened, just a little. "Shuck 'em—"

"Suck 'em," he finished. Once, a local down in Playa del Carmen had actually offered to buy that shirt right off his back. "That's the one."

"I'm pretty sure it's there," she said.

He nodded. "I'll take a look." But he didn't move to do so, couldn't. "Meg, I…" The words thickened on the way out. "I'm sorry I wasn't at Dr. Brennan's that day."

Her eyes widened, darkened. Had he ever said that? He thought he had. Surely he had.

"I know," she whispered.

It was not what he expected her to say.

"I tried to get out of my meeting—"

"It wouldn't have changed anything." She glanced down at the crocheted booties, running her thumb gently along the bottoms.

The churning in his stomach was as familiar as it was foreign. He'd taught himself much since he'd packed his daughter's room into boxes and hauled them into the attic: how to let go, how to say goodbye. How to move on. Some had come easy. Most had not.

"You really believe that?" he asked.

She picked up the booties and set them gently into the big pink box, setting the matching blanket on top. "She'd still be gone."

The quiet words, the truth of them, punished. "But you wouldn't have been alone." That had always haunted him, the thought of her lying there alone on that cold exam table, waiting to find out whether their child was a boy or a girl, only to have Dr. Brennan frown as she turned the screen away.

Meg had never spoken of it. What he knew, he knew from her doctor—and from Lori.

And he'd always wondered. If he'd been there, if he'd been by her side, holding her hand, could he have changed something, kept her from slipping away?

The next time he *had* been there, when they'd tried IVF. He'd gone to every appointment, never let go of her hand, even when it was cold and limp. He'd been there when Dr. Brennan called with the results of the pregnancy test.

Two weeks later he'd boarded a plane for Africa.

"Don't blame yourself," Meg said, returning the rest of the little clothes to the box.

God, he hoped she didn't come up here often.

"Sometimes things just happen," she added as she snapped the lid into place.

He knew that. "I just didn't want you to hurt."

Through the shadows, her smile was soft—wistful. "I didn't want that for you, either."

Something inside him tightened. He wanted to be angry, to be incredulous that she who'd wielded the knife could be so philosophical about it all now. But she'd hurt, too, he knew. She'd suffered. He could see it in her eyes, a wariness, a regret that went deeper than the grief he'd seen before.

He could see it every time he saw her with Charlotte.

"She'd be almost two years old."

The quiet words rocked him. The way she knelt there in the shadows, feathering her hand along the top of the tub—gentle, soothing—punished. "I know."

His words were as quiet, as devastated, as hers.

Through the stillness, a faraway smile touched Meg's face. "I think about her sometimes."

"So do I."

Her eyes lifted to his, and in them he wasn't sure if he saw surprise—or gratitude.

"I think about what she would look like," he went on. "Her smile. How her voice would sound." How different their lives could have been.

"You," Meg said, surprising him. "She would have looked like you."

The vise around Russell's chest tightened. "I don't think so," he muttered. "When she comes to me in my dreams, I see—"

Her.

Meg.

The memory all but eviscerated him, the sound of that sweet little voice, the joy contained in one simple word. *Dada…* Through the darkness she'd call out to him, *for him,* and he'd turn toward her, see her there, standing in a veil of mist not too far away, a precious little girl with curly blond hair and enormous blue eyes. She'd lift her hands to him, he'd lift his to her.

But at the moment before he touched her, he always woke up.

Cold.

Alone.

"Russell?"

Yanking himself back, he found Meg standing, moving toward him. Her face was pale, her eyes dark. Her gaze searched his. "What, Russell? What do you see?"

He stiffened, shaking off the unwanted shards of memory.

"When you dream," she whispered. "What do you see when you dream?"

He looked at her standing in the shadows cast by the lantern, surrounded by neatly stacked tubs and crates of a lifetime that had somehow slipped away, and all he could think was…who was this woman? Who was this woman who spoke and listened, who asked questions… and answered them?

It was the most honest conversation they'd had in more than two years. Maybe ever.

"Do you really want me to answer that?" he asked,

and his words were quiet. Hoarse. With them, his body tensed.

Her eyes darkened. Her mouth parted, just as it had earlier, when he'd reached for her. When time had fallen away and want had poured in, when need had taken over and their mouths had come together.

She lifted her arms and for a moment he tensed, shocked that she was going to touch him again. But she didn't. She hugged her arms around herself, rocked back.

"I better check on Charlotte," she said, and before he could so much as blink she was slipping past him, just as she always did, sweeping the moment of naked honesty under the rug. Erasing it. Just as she'd erased so much else...anything and everything that made her uncomfortable.

With the rain splattering against the old roof, something dark and punishing pounded through him. He picked up one of the tubs of his old clothes, yanked the cord to the lantern and headed downstairs.

"CALL ME BACK IF HER FEVER gets over 101."

"Okay, but—"

"Meg." Dr. Darla Graham's voice was warm but firm. "I know you're worried, but trust me, babies get fevers. I know it's scary for you, but give her a few hours. If she's not better in the morning, call me back."

Meg kneeled by the sofa, having come down from the attic to find the baby's forehead warmer than usual, but not burning up.

"I'm sorry," she said, acutely aware of how neurotic she was being, but grateful for the pediatrician's patience. They'd crossed paths once before Charlotte had come along, at one of her cousin Faith's infamous backyard bashes, but for the most part, it was a whole new world of doctors and playdates, nannies and baby stores and toys. Lots and lots of toys. "I'm just new at this."

"Of course you are," Darla said. "It comes with the territory."

Meg soothed a damp strawberry curl back from Charlotte's face as a streak of lightning brightened the room. "Then when will I relax?"

Darla laughed. "Oh, maybe about the time she hits thirty."

With the rumble of thunder, Meg smiled, marveling that anyone could sleep through the spring storm. "Okay—101 or higher, call you. Otherwise…chill out."

"You can call me anyway," Darla said. "Just try to relax."

"Got it." They said their goodbyes and Meg put down the phone, watching the baby sleep. She looked peaceful, curled on her side with her hands tucked up under her chin. That had to be a good sign, that she wasn't thrashing the way she had the last time she had a fever. That night, Meg had gone dusk to dawn without sleep.

Out of the corner of her eye, she caught movement from the kitchen and looked up to find Russell with a wineglass in each hand.

"Here," he said, offering one to her.

The stab was as sharp as it was unexpected. She pushed to her feet and crossed to him, met him before he could reach the edge of the old braided rug. "I thought you were leaving."

"Wanted to see what the doctor said first."

Meg eyed the glass in his hands. "She said not to worry."

"And did you tell her that wasn't possible?"

"Something like that." She wasn't sure she'd relaxed for more than a minute or two since Charlotte had come to live with her. "I thought I knew, you know? I thought I knew what love was."

She regretted her choice of words the second they left her mouth.

"I mean…I used to worry about you—a car accident, some sudden illness, a dangerous assignment—but it was always fleeting, one of those nasty thoughts you can push aside. But Charlotte…"

"*Meggie.* You're doing great."

"Maybe it's because of Hope," she said, glancing from Russell to the sofa, where Charlotte still slept, her bright red hair damp against her flushed face. "Because of the way we lost her. Before then, things just worked out, even with my mother. Not everyone survives breast cancer. But she did. And then there was the infertility, but we overcame that, too. We even got through the first trimester! But then she just…died. She was just gone, Russell, and I couldn't fix that."

"It wasn't your fault."

"I know that! But then you were gone and Ainsley was dead, and suddenly Charlotte was here, and all I could think was, *'Oh, my God, what if something happens to her?'*"

"Nothing is going to happen to Charlotte."

"But babies die, Russell. It happens. Julia had a younger sister…did you know that? She died of SIDS when she was seven months old. My aunt was pregnant with Faith at the time—that's how she got her name."

"Meg—"

"And I just…sometimes it overwhelms me. I've got this precious little life in my hands, and if anything ever happened to her… Sometimes when she sleeps I just stand there and watch her, hang on every breath.…"

"How could you not?" he said with a tenderness she hadn't heard from him in a very long time. "Come on," he said, offering her the goblet again. "Why don't you sit and rest for a while—you're exhausted."

She looked at the glass in his hand—a hand where a wedding ring had once resided. Against the handblown crystal, the dark burgundy sloshed—the same dark burgundy she'd put back on the shelf the night before—and everything inside her tensed. Her mouth went dry… then started to water. The glass was so close. All she had to do was take it, draw it to her lips. One sip. That was all.

One sip wouldn't hurt anything.

"Meg?" he asked, and through the fog she heard the confusion in his voice. "You weren't saving that bottle for something special, were you?"

She forced her eyes to his and felt the odd rush clear down to her toes, just like in the attic, when he'd asked if she wanted to know what he saw in his dreams.

The thought had swirled through her, as warm and seductive as the first sip of wine. Russell in bed… naked.

He always slept naked.

She jerked herself back, just as she'd done in the attic. They'd been speaking of Hope, their child. Instead, Meg had seen Russell sprawled on a big bed, wrapped in a crisp cotton sheet.

The realization still disturbed her.

"I need to stay alert," she said, stepping back. "I

don't need..." Help. *Him*. "I just want to get to bed."
She verbally detoured, but when the green of his eyes
went dark, she realized her mistake.

This had been their house. They'd lived here, loved
here. It was only natural that seeing him here would
stir up old feelings—and dreams.

That's why she'd kissed him. That's why she'd
reached for him, opened to him.

Wanted him.

It had been so long.

"Please," she said, and even as she formed the word,
she had to wonder what she meant. What she wanted.

Why he wouldn't just *leave?* The irony was not lost
on her. The one time she wanted him gone, he turned
into glue.

"You should go." The festival was only a few days
away. She had a ton of work to get done. She so did not
have time to play house with the one man who could
destroy it all. *Again.*

Through the recessed lighting, his eyes seemed to
glow. "Or maybe I should stay," he said. "Let you get
some rest."

"Russell—"

"Charlotte has a fever, may not sleep well. Why don't
you just let me stand point so you can crawl into bed
and get some real sleep?"

"No." The word shot out of her. The offer was like
vinegar on a healing wound. "We're fine—I can take
care of Charlotte."

"Of course you can," he said. "But with the
storm—"

"Russell." Instinct, self-preservation, they both told
her to get him out of there before she did something

she'd regret. "I'm hardly someone who needs my hand held during a thunderstorm."

"I know." His voice was warm, rich like the wine he'd offered her. It seeped through her, coercing her to relax, even as she warned herself not to. "I remember."

So did she. Closing her eyes, she saw it all, the summer day a lifetime before, when a world-weary Russell Montgomery had walked back into her life after she'd been forced to leave New York. Months had passed since they'd seen each other. She'd been caring for her mother. He'd been off covering another war. There'd been the occasional e-mail, but no phone calls.

Then she'd looked up from her desk at the paper one day, and he'd been there, bigger than life, lounging in the doorway with a backpack slung over his shoulder, watching her. Just watching her. As he always had, with that secret, intimate gleam in his eyes.

And everything inside her had started to melt.

It was all a blur after that. She stood. He moved. They met somewhere in the middle. His arms around her. Hers around him. The feel of him pressed up against her, his mouth slanting against hers. She held on tight, holding him, loving the feel of him, shocked that he'd come for her, never wanting to let go.

Somehow they'd made it back to his room at the Magnolia Manor.

It had been spring then, too. There'd been thunder in the distance when they came together for the first time, making love in broad daylight…in a hotel rumored to be haunted.

There'd been so many other springs since then, so many other storms. So many other afternoons spent making love. In their bed, beneath the fall of the old willow out back by the creek...on the kitchen floor.

Opening her eyes, she found him watching her much as he'd watched her the day he'd come for her, all those months after she'd been forced to leave New York. There was a stillness to him now, an intensity that snaked through her with carnal precision. Both wineglasses were still in his hands, untouched.

Looking at him hurt. Remembering...ached.

Because she didn't know what else to do, she slipped past him and headed to the front door, let herself onto the slightly chilly, rain-splattered front porch, where at least she could breathe without pulling the scent of him deep, deep within her.

She felt him before she heard the squeak of the screen door.

"We always did better with the storms around us," she whispered as the damp wind whipped her hair against her face, "than the storms inside."

He closed the distance between them, moving to stand behind her, his hands clutching the rail on either side of her. All she had to do was close her eyes and lean back....

"Sometimes, luv, you just have to let the clouds clear."

Luv. God, when was the last time he'd called her that?

Not trusting herself to look back, Meg looked past the truck parked across the street to the house beyond, the glow of lights from every window in the Victorian house.

"Why did you walk away?"

She stilled. Around her the heavily leafed branches of the oaks swayed with the storm, horizontal flashes of lightning illuminating the riot of rain. But she did not let herself move.

She'd never gone anywhere.

"In the attic," Russell clarified, and his voice was oddly hoarse. "Why did you walk away?"

CHAPTER EIGHT

Eleven months before

THE LIGHTS WERE LOW, the music loud. From the jukebox, Faith Hill sang about melting and floating and breathing...and love.

It was the fourth time Meg had selected the same song.

She sat at a back table in the smoky honky-tonk, watching. Numb. Around her the scene was the same as it was the week before: women in tight jeans and tighter shirts, shiny silver-and-turquoise belt buckles, some with hats, most in boots. Perfect hair. Perfect smiles.

Perfect...everything.

The men, in their low-slung jeans and Western shirts and scuffed-up boots, moved among them, offering up drinks and dances and...more.

Alone, Meg glanced at the wineglass on the table in front of her. The paper was in trouble. Advertisers were bailing. Circulation was down. The staff had been cut, and cut, and cut some more. Just that afternoon she'd had to let three more go, including Marlene, who'd been with the *Gazette* for over fifty years. And with each severance package, with each teary goodbye, something inside Meg screamed a little louder. If she couldn't get a handle on—

"You're back." The drawl was low, husky. Before

Meg could so much as blink, the stranger pulled out the chair next to her and slid in close. "I got you another," he said, easing a fresh glass of wine near her hands. Slowly, his eyes met hers. "Didn't think a pretty thing like you should drink alone."

Meg knew she should say something. Feel something. Do something. That's how the game was played. But inside, the web of numbness spread deeper.

"Name is Cody," the man said with a slow, intimate smile. His face was tanned, slightly leathery, with a dark shadow at his jaw. His hair was thick, wavy, the kind a woman liked to run her hands through. "Been hoping you would come back."

She eyed the glass of wine. Just one sip, she thought. Just one more sip…

"You look surprised," Cody said, and then his hand was on her wrist, softly, gently, fingers stroking flesh, his thumb strumming a faint little circle. "And sad," he murmured, inching closer. "Far too sad for such a pretty lady."

The words washed over her. She reached for them, pulled them close. Wanted them.

Wanted them so damn bad.

It had been…she didn't know. She'd lost track of time. But she knew it had been a long time since she'd felt a man's touch. When she closed her eyes, Russell's face was barely more than a shadowy memory, his voice like fading smoke. His touch…

She no longer remembered his touch.

Refusing to linger, she reached for the fresh glass of wine and drew it to her mouth. Sipped slowly. Deeply.

All the while she kept her eyes on Cody's, on the hunger burning in his.

A hunger she had not seen in a very long time.
A hunger she wanted desperately to feel again.

Present Day

EACH FLASH OF LIGHTNING gave a glimpse into the night, the frenzy of the rain, the way the branches whipped and bushes shook. Water streamed down the driveway and swirled in the street, gathering faster than it could drain away. New foliage lay among the hail-flattened petunias Meg had planted a few weeks before.

Funny. She hadn't even noticed the hail. In fact, she'd almost forgotten Russell was waiting for an answer to his question.

Why had she walked away from the attic? That was easy.

"I was worried about Charlotte," she said, trying not to shiver. Only that afternoon the temperature had soared into the low eighties. She was quite sure the storm had dropped the mercury a good twenty degrees since then.

"But that's not why you walked away, is it?"

A screen surrounded the porch, but the wind blew the rain sideways, sending it like tiny stinging missiles toward the house. Meg braced herself against the onslaught, even as the chill crept deeper.

"This is me you're talking to, Meg. Me. *Your husband.* And I know what you're doing."

Against the rail, her hands tightened, but she said nothing.

"You had me in there. You really did. Telling me your fears, your dreams, but the second it starts getting real, the second you think you might hear something you don't want to, you run as fast and far as you can."

She'd realized her mistake the second she'd asked him about his dreams. She'd just gotten so caught up in the moment and the memories, for a moment there it had just been her and Russell. Once, dreams had not been taboo.

"I walked away," she said very coolly, very slowly, "because it doesn't matter."

"*Goddamn it,* Meg." And then his hands were on her body, not gentle like before, but forceful enough to make her turn toward him. "*Stop,* okay? The games… the pretending…that's what doesn't matter now, not anymore. Can't you be honest with yourself, with me, even now?"

"You want honesty?" she asked, and it all boiled up inside her, the honesty and the heartache, the nights she'd sat up alone, with nothing but a bottle of wine to offer her company. "I'll give you honesty. I don't want this, Russell. I don't want to know what you dream about, I don't want to stroll down memory lane, and I don't want *you*." There was too much water under the bridge. "I've worked hard to move on with my life, to run the paper and take care of Charlotte. Looking back…no good can come from it."

"What about forward?"

She glanced at his hands, still against her upper arms. "Where is your next assignment? When do you leave?"

The lines of his face tightened.

"That's forward," she said. "That's what tomorrow holds."

His hands fell away. He stepped back. "I see her." His voice, flat, empty, slammed into Meg like the challenge it was. "I see our little girl."

Meg stilled, didn't want to hear.

But he kept right on going, doing what she'd asked him not to do, as if somehow he magically knew what was best for her.

Just like before.

"Laughing," he said, and the image immediately formed, the one that had haunted Meg since the moment she'd seen Dr. Brennan's face cloud over.

"I see you," he said, his words barely audible over the wind. "What could have been."

If Hope hadn't died.

The coldness came faster now, sharper, no longer seeping but slicing with debilitating precision. "Russell, don't."

"Don't what?"

It was all she could do not to charge him, to throw her hands against his chest and push him away, make him leave. "Why are *you* doing this?"

But he was so damn calm. So damn in control. "No, Meg, why are you doing this?"

She wanted to scream. It was impossible to have a conversation with someone who commandeered every question and made it their own. "Doing what?"

"What you always do," he said in a voice she instantly recognized, the one that was deceptively calm and civilized. The one that always meant the ax was about to fall. "Checking on Charlotte, rearranging the pantry, going to bed without telling me or staying up late to work on some important project so you don't have to endure me touching you…it's all the same, Meg. It's all hiding—pretending, playing by some set of rules you never bothered to tell me about."

"That's not fair."

"No, it wasn't. Jesus Christ, Meg, I was your husband, but every time I so much as touched you, you cringed as if I was a pervert or something."

She stood there, absorbed the sting of his words.

"Do you have any idea what that did to me?"

"To you?" she shot back. "I was the one trying like hell to hold myself together, when all you could think about was how long it had been since we had sex."

"Sex." He physically reeled, as if she'd just knifed him in the gut. "I was hurting, too, Meg. Did it ever occur to you I needed my wife?"

"And I needed time."

Through the strobe light of the storm, he looked so very tall standing there on the front porch, rain sliding down the lines of his cheeks, his body perfectly still. The light in his eyes completely gone. "Looks like you got what you wanted then. Congratulations."

He didn't wait for her to say anything—she wasn't sure what there was to say. He turned from her as if she was something ugly and broken and crossed the porch, his loafers coming down in hard splashes against the puddles. He reached the rail, yanked open the screen door, strode into the rain.

Meg stood on the porch for a long, long time, watching taillights disappear in the storm. Even then she remained, watching, unable to turn away, walk away.

Until Charlotte started to cry.

"DID HE SPEND THE NIGHT?"

Seated at the big curved booth at the back of Uncle Ralph's, Meg reached for her water glass. The lunch crowd had thinned, leaving only one other table occupied. "Of course not."

"I love the way you say that," Julia said, plucking a tortilla chip from the basket in the center of the table.

"*Of course not.* Like why would I ask such a crazy question?" With a pointed smile, she scooped the little triangle into the freshly made guacamole. "Because it's not like you waited two days to even mention it to us or anything," she pressed on, the way only she could. "Your husband in your kitchen...naked."

Husband. The word made Meg shift uncomfortably against the vinyl cushion.

"He was wearing a blanket," Lori pointed out, gnawing on a chip of her own. "Or at least that's what Meg *says.*"

Meg glanced around for Ruby, who was apparently in no hurry to clear out the stragglers. "I don't know why I even said anything."

"Because for two days you've been somewhere far, far away," Julia said. "Now we know where."

"It was no big deal—he was just watching Charlotte for a few hours."

"*Naked,*" Julia reminded.

"Seriously," Meg said as her cell phone beeped the arrival of a text message. "Can you just forget I even mentioned that?"

God knew she was trying to forget the whole thing.

Julia, being Julia, refused to back down. "Can you?"

Sighing, Meg knew the answer to both questions. No. She couldn't forget any more than Julia and Lori could. God knew she'd tried.

"I bet he's still got that killer chest, too, doesn't he?" Lori said, and with the simple question the image formed, Russell lounging in the entryway to the kitchen, his body big and hard and naked except for that little yellow...loincloth.

Quickly Meg reached for her purse, fumbling for her BlackBerry. The last thing she needed was for her friends to see her eyes—or the flush she couldn't prevent. Because then they would know there was so much more than Meg was telling them.

They knew anyway. "Something happened, didn't it?" Julia asked. "That's why you've been holding out on us."

"We talked." If you could call that talking.

"Talked. About what?"

Meg closed her fingers around her phone. "Hope," she said. "Dreams." Sex.

Or the serious lack thereof.

I was hurting, too, Meg. Did it ever occur to you I needed my wife?

Even now, his words, the raw humiliation in his eyes, haunted her. Almost forty-eight hours had passed since she'd asked him to leave. During that time there'd been nothing. No sightings. No phone calls.

No signed divorce papers.

Frowning, she unlocked the phone and pulled up the text message from one of her editorial assistants.

Ur 1:30 is waiting.

Three minutes later, she was hurrying across the street. She'd checked her calendar that morning, but through the rush of meetings since then had forgotten about the appointment Lori had added after Meg left the afternoon before. Lori said the young man had been insistent about seeing Meg.

Kids from the community college came in all the time, eager for a job. Meg didn't have any openings, but it never hurt to hear what they had to say.

"Hi," Meg said, breezing into the sun-dappled outer office. She saw him sitting rigidly on the dainty camel-back sofa her grandfather had placed in that exact spot half a century before.

"I'm Meg," she said in greeting. "I understand you want to see me?"

The young man with closely cropped hair stood, his jeans faded and his white T-shirt wrinkled, but his posture ramrod straight. "Hi," he said with an endearing awkwardness. His smile was warm, but unsure somehow. "I'm Tyler."

Extending a hand, Meg closed the distance between them. There was something vaguely familiar about him...that smile, but she couldn't place him. "Have we met before?"

He took her hand and shook it briefly, quickly. "No, but Ainsley—"

Meg stilled, all but her heart. It started to pound.
Tyler.

The name drifted through her, stripping away the weeks and the months, to the spring day shortly after Russell left, when she and Ainsley had walked among the willows at the edge of the creek behind Meg's house. Ainsley had practically floated. Her eyes had glowed.

"You knew Ainsley?" Her throat locked around the words, but even before the question found voice, she remembered the picture in Ainsley's bedroom, and knew the answer.

"Before I left for Iraq," Tyler was saying as the memories kept piling onto one another, the first blush of love, the excitement and the tears...the nights Meg had held a sobbing Ainsley. The morning they'd both stared at the positive pregnancy test.

"I got back last month," he said. "I tried to find her,

didn't understand why she'd quit writing." He hesitated, his gaze distant, devastated. "I thought maybe she got tired of waiting."

The pain in his voice stirred something deep inside her. "No," she said, reaching for him again, taking his hands and squeezing. "She never got tired of waiting."

"When I found her number disconnected, I thought maybe she was telling me to get lost. But I did an Internet search…" His eyes, an intelligent piercing blue, filled. "I found her obituary."

And Meg couldn't do it. She couldn't just stand there in a slant of sunlight while Ainsley's soldier fell apart in front of her. Instinct took over and she stepped toward him, put her arms around him and closed her eyes. "I'm so sorry."

She thought maybe he would just stand there, wooden, like the soldier he was. He didn't. He sank into her more like a child than a man, his arms closing around her and holding on. Sobs shuddered through the solid strength of his body. "There was a write-up in the *Gazette,*" he muttered—and Meg's throat became even tighter.

Over the years she'd written hundreds of obituaries and tributes and accident reports. But that morning she'd just sat there at her laptop, her eyes blurring, her fingers frozen. Julia had offered to take over.

Meg had refused. She'd owed her sister-in-law that final courtesy…just as she owed her so much more.

"Did she…" Tyler pulled back so that his eyes met Meg's. "Did she suffer?"

Meg swallowed, searched for words. "No," she lied, seeing her sister-in-law's final moments all over again, the agony, the tortured glow of awareness. Ainsley had known she was dying. She'd known she was leaving her little girl behind.

She'd known she would never see Tyler again.

"She whispered your name," Meg said quietly, as a fresh wash of pain twisted across Tyler's face. "She wanted you to know that she loved you."

His throat worked. "And the baby?"

Meg froze. Her hands remained on Tyler's shoulders, her gaze on his face, a face so staggeringly familiar, considering she'd never seen him before. She'd always thought Charlotte the spitting image of Russell, but there was no denying that the young man standing inches from her was, in fact, Charlotte's father. The almond shape of the eyes, the rounded bow of his top lip, the endearing little lopsided smile...

"I—I...saw her," he said.

The quick knife of panic went deep. "You *saw* her?"

"Around town," Tyler said. "I've been here a few days. I had to see her...I had to know."

Somehow Meg remained standing. Somehow she held it all together, while inside everything unraveled. Tyler had been watching them. He'd seen Charlotte. He knew. He knew she was his daughter.

"I'd like to see her," he said, stepping back from Meg and going all soldier-straight again, the boy vanishing, the man, the father, standing tall. "I think she's mine."

THE SPARKLY PINK BALL zoomed down the narrow Wii alley, curving just a fraction toward the end. There it slammed perfectly into the side of the middle pin, knocking all ten of them down.

"Look at you!" Russell said as a voice from the television announced, *"Nice throw!"*

Meg's mother beamed. "It's all in the wrist," she said.

But Russell didn't think so. This was their third game. So far he'd been pretty good at picking up spares, but strikes had eluded him. Lilah had dubbed him King of the Splits.

"Just pretend like you're at the bowling alley," she coached, as she'd been doing from the start. "Pretend like you're really throwing a ball."

Standing about five feet back from the massive plasma TV, in a room otherwise dominated by Victorian finery and heavy velvet drapes, Russell sent his mother-in-law a playful smile. "Come on, Mama Lilah." She'd always insisted that he call her that. "You know I've never been very good at pretending."

She frowned. "Sometimes you got to," she said, reaching past one of the three huge Siamese cats for her glass of raspberry green tea. She guzzled the stuff by the gallon, had since her cancer diagnosis. "Sometimes it's the only way to get to the other side."

Frowning, Russell positioned his Mii character and lifted his arm, initiated his swing and stepped forward, just as he'd done countless times before, when he and Meg had killed time at the local bowling alley. The blue ball shot down the narrow alley, perfectly straight until just before the end. There it hooked sharply and knocked only the three pins farthest to the left.

"You're not letting yourself see it," Lilah said. As if it was as natural as breathing, she put down her tea and positioned herself in front of the TV, initiated her swing and once again knocked down every pin. "You have to trust," she said, clearly pleased with herself. "You have to see what you want, not where you are."

Subtlety was not Lilah Roberts's forte.

He'd debated the wisdom of stopping by. She was Meg's mother. They were tight. He couldn't imagine he was too high on her list of favorite people.

But she'd answered his call on the second ring and invited him straight over. She'd opened the door before he'd had a chance to knock. And then she'd hugged him. Just hugged him.

In the end, it was as simple as that.

"Always knew you'd be back," she'd said when she'd finally pulled away. "Always knew someday the same winds that blew you here in the first place would blow you back."

"So what *do* you want, Russell Paul?" She'd always called him that. "That's what it all comes down to."

His own mother was sturdy and practical…she'd had to be. With a brood of nine children, there'd been no time for games—or meditation. Lilah had always been a breath of fresh air.

"Your daughter wants me gone," he said, deliberately lining up his next shot so he didn't have to see Lilah's eyes—and so she didn't see his.

She humphed. "First off, that's not what I asked you. Secondly, though…can you blame her? Most folks don't take a shine to walking on broken glass."

He stared at the sweet big-screen television, still trying to absorb that it belonged to Meg's mother. Then he swung back and killed the ball. It bounced once before barreling down the video alley, smashing into the remaining pins.

"Nice spare!" the console narrated.

Lilah remained a few steps behind and to the right

of him, one hand stroking the cat perched on the arm of a deep purple camelback sofa. On the dainty end table just a few feet away sat his and Meg's wedding picture.

"Try again," she said. "You, Russell Paul Montgomery. What do *you* want?"

It was a bloody good question. Not that long ago, he'd been sure he knew. Out in the field, on assignment, doing what he did. Watching. Observing. Documenting.

Packing up, moving on.

Before then, the answer had been easy.

He'd wanted Meg. A family. The future.

"I'm due back in Afghanistan next week."

All brisk and businesslike, Lilah lined up her next shot. "And I'll be in Peru," she said. "I've wanted to go as long as I can remember, to see Machu Picchu with my own eyes. Thought I had Ray talked into it, but the old coot's hell-bent on never taking a breath outside of Texas." Hesitating, she launched her shot—and once again smoked the pins.

"So now that we know our travel plans," she said, turning to scorch him with one of her patented pecan-pie-sweet smiles, "you gonna answer my question?"

It was the damnedest thing. Lilah went straight to the meat of the matter. There was no skirting around the issue, no running or hiding. She just laid it all out there.

He'd never understood why Meg couldn't do the same.

"Okay, apparently not," Lilah said, sweeping a strand of silver hair from her face. Most of it was secured in a long braid down her back. Silver hoops dangled from her ears. A gorgeous turquoise pendant lay against her chest. "Let me tell you something, Russell. I was supposed to die. I still will, of course. But not yet."

She'd kicked stage-two breast cancer. She'd endured a double mastectomy, chemo and radiation, but never once had Russell heard her feel the least bit sorry for herself.

"But you know what? Having a doctor look you in the eye and say the word *cancer,* going on the Internet and reading all the statistics and horror stories, meeting women in treatment, then going to their funerals…it changes you. It teaches you, brings life into this razor-sharp focus that can cut to the bone." She hesitated, her hand fluttering down to find Simon's back. The sleek cat with marble blue eyes had not been here the last time Russell visited Lilah. "There's only one way to live, my nomad son-in-law, and that's without regrets.

"Go to Afghanistan, if that's what you want to do. Take your pictures," she said as his cell phone started to ring. "Just make sure you know why you're there."

On the television screen, his Mii character waited for him to make his move, while Lilah's character bobbed in the background.

"Best answer that," she said. "Never know when it's the one that matters."

THE DRIVE ACROSS TOWN felt like an eternity. Meg pulled into her driveway, glancing in the rearview mirror to see Tyler pull in behind her—in the white truck she'd seen parked across the street off and on over the past week.

She wasn't sure which unnerved her more—the realization that he'd been watching them, or the fact that she, a trained journalist, had been completely oblivious.

She parked and slipped out of the car, met him at the front porch. "I have a nanny," she explained, reaching for the screen door. "A friend of my mother's, Miss Rosemary, stays with Charlotte."

"She's real good with her," Tyler said, and Meg's unease skittered a little deeper. No, she wanted to scream. *No! Go away. Stay away from my daughter!*

Except Charlotte wasn't hers.

"Yes, she is," Meg murmured, sliding the key into the lock when the screech of tires had her glancing toward the street.

The blue sedan zipped around the corner, jerking to a quick stop in front of her house. And then the door swung open and Russell materialized, shoving the door shut as he started toward the house.

CHAPTER NINE

THE IRRATIONAL FLASH of relief almost made Meg's legs buckle. Meg watched him cross the front yard, striding onto the porch and closing in on them as if he had every right to be there.

As if he belonged.

Two days before, he'd walked away. She'd all but shoved him. Now he came right up to them, taking his place by Meg's side and sliding an arm around her waist in silent solidarity, urging her against him. Into him.

She didn't resist. *"Russell,"* she said, hating how thin her voice sounded. How...scared. "This is—"

"I know." The lines of his face hardened as he sized up the young man who'd knocked up his sister...then left her alone. "Lori called me."

Tyler's eyes flared. Clearly he knew who Russell was, too. No doubt Ainsley had told him a thing or two about the take-no-prisoners brother she worshipped.

"I understand you want to see Charlotte," Russell said, cutting straight to the chase.

Tyler nodded, cleared his throat before speaking. "I do."

Around her waist, Russell's arm tightened. "My sister loved you, you know," he said, and at the protective edge to his voice, Meg's eyes stung all over again. He'd loved his baby sister...had been there for her even when thousands of miles had separated them.

Even as the truth hurt, something soft and fragile bloomed within Meg. She was glad of that, glad that he'd been there for Ainsley, that some bonds really did last forever.

"I wanted to marry her," Tyler said, and from the pain in his bloodshot eyes, it was clear that he spoke the truth.

Together, Meg and Russell led Ainsley's soldier into the cool shadows of the house. And together, they stepped into the backyard, where Rosemary pushed a giggling Charlotte in a baby swing hanging from one of the towering old post oaks. Russell reached for Meg's hand. She welcomed the warmth, held on. Silently they crossed the grass, Tyler a few steps behind.

"Well, this is surely a nice surprise," Rosemary said, beaming as she reached to stop the swing. Charlotte, completely recovered from her two-day bout with a fever, clapped her hands.

And Meg's heart just shattered.

Curved around her hand, Russell's fingers tightened, but she didn't return the gesture, couldn't. Couldn't look at him, even though she felt the burn of his gaze. Couldn't move. Couldn't breathe. Could only watch Tyler move forward, his face ashen, his smile so tender it hurt.

Russell urged her closer, released her hand to again anchor an arm around her waist.

"She's beautiful," Tyler said, reaching the swing.

Always the socialite, Charlotte started to babble, lifting a chubby little hand to grab at the one Tyler extended.

"Just like her mom," he muttered, as the warm breeze played with two miniature pigtails of shockingly red hair. And Meg didn't know how much longer she could do it, how much longer she could stand there frozen in the whisper of the old post oaks, watching father and daughter smile in discovery.

"Do you want to hold her?" The question came out before Meg could stop it. Offering just seemed like the right thing to do. Tyler, this boy on the verge of manhood, *was* Charlotte's father.

He froze, much as Russell had done the week before, when Meg had asked him the very same question. This time Russell stepped forward, finagling his niece free of the swing and anchoring her squirmy body against his side.

Mine, the gesture screamed.

"Dada-dada," Charlotte cooed, not really to Russell, Meg knew—it was just one of the few sounds she could make.

Tyler paled anyway, his expression going blank as Russell ran his fingers along Charlotte's tummy, and she in turn dissolved into full baby belly laughs. "I—I…"

Meg watched Tyler take a step back, wondered if he even realized that he'd moved. It was a lot to take in. Returning from Iraq, finding the girl he loved dead, discovering that he'd fathered a child.

"I gotta go," he said, looking from his daughter to Meg, his eyes dark, devastated. "I don't want to—" trancelike, his gaze went back to his flirty little daughter cooing madly at her uncle "—scare her."

And then he turned and walked away with that ramrod perfect posture that screamed of his time in service to his country.

Instinctively Meg wondered what it cost him not to run.

"THERE'S MY GIRL," MEG SAID, propping Charlotte on wobbly legs against a wall, then easing back a few feet. "Show me what you can do."

Big, almond-shaped green eyes danced with excitement. The baby lifted her arms toward Meg and leaned forward, extended one leg…then fell to her hands and knees.

"Good girl!" Meg praised, picking Charlotte up and giving her a quick kiss to her forehead before returning her to the wall. She was so close to taking those first few steps on her own. "Let's try again."

Charlotte giggled, sliding down to land on her diaper-clad bottom.

"Tired?" Meg asked, scooping the baby up and drawing her in for a full-body hug. "You've been working so hard."

Charlotte squirmed, twisting free to take off in a mad crawl for a stack of blocks across the family room.

The hot, salty sting against Meg's eyes was immediate. She rocked back and watched, didn't know how she'd ever say goodbye. From the moment she'd first seen Charlotte, the connection had been there. Those innocent eyes had glowed with what could only be described as a wisdom, a silent, unmistakable recognition, as if the freshly born baby was somehow saying, *"Oh, it's you! What took you so long?"*

Charlotte was Ainsley's. Meg had always known that. But from the very start her niece had brought light to all those dark places in Meg's heart, even when Meg only saw her every few days.

But the past two months…

Meg closed her eyes as her heart squeezed.

"You okay?"

Wiping at her face, she twisted around to find Russell

standing in the back doorway. His thick copper hair was mussed from the breeze, his face hard, his eyes narrow, concentrated on her like a spotlight. He'd stepped outside after Rosemary left, excusing himself to make a phone call.

She'd not heard him come back in, wasn't sure why he was still there.

It hurt to look at him. It hurt to see him standing in the shadows just inside the back porch, the way he'd done so many times before. It hurt to think about how far in the past that was.

"He's coming back," she said, shifting her glance to Charlotte, who was busily retrieving play cookies from a pretend cookie jar, then shoving them back in.

Russell moved deeper into the room, not toward Charlotte, but Meg. "You don't know that. He's just a kid."

Kids went to war, Meg knew. It happened every day. But kids didn't come back. Men did.

"Doesn't matter," she said, wiping her palms against the black cargo pants she'd changed into after Tyler left. Part of her wanted to scoop the baby up and run, run far. *Hide.*

Before her whole world was ripped apart.

But one simple truth kept her standing beside the sofa, even as the cold bleed of inevitability seeped through her.

"She's his," she said. "How do you walk away from something like that?"

Beside her, Russell stiffened. And when he spoke, his voice was quiet. "Sometimes you have to. It's either that or you suffocate."

Her throat burned. She could feel him standing there,

feel the tension of his body, but knew better than to look. Didn't want to see.

"It wasn't like she was conceived through some one-night stand," she pointed out, hating the twist of vulnerability those words caused her. It didn't make any sense that she could want him to walk away, even as she wanted him to take her in his arms again, to hold on tight and never let go.

Residual feelings, she told herself. Pesky little loose ends that had never been properly cauterized.

"Ainsley was crazy about him," she whispered as Charlotte looked up and started to clap.

Russell let out a rough breath, one Meg instantly recognized as frustration. "I know that," he said. "And God knows I tried to get her to tell him about the baby."

So had Meg. But Ainsley had been insistent. So long as Tyler was fighting in a faraway land, she didn't want to be the cause of any distractions. She wanted him to focus on the job he was doing, and then come home to her.

"She was going to," Meg said, going down on her knees and stacking a few wooden alphabet blocks. "When he got back." She paused, let the memory wash over her. "She talked about it all the time. Dreamed about it, him."

Charlotte, in a cute little flowered top and matching pink bloomers Meg had spent way too much money on, stopped what she was doing and powered over, lifting a hand to demolish the tower Meg had just made.

Smiling wasn't supposed to hurt. "She had it all planned out—what she would say to him, what his reaction would be." Hesitating, she leaned forward to restack the blocks. "What it would be like to see her little girl in her daddy's arms for the first time."

"Meg."

She didn't know what to do with the concern in Russell's voice, especially after all the things she'd said to him just a few nights before.

So she pretended she didn't hear it. "It's what your sister wanted," she said as Charlotte once again swatted at the blocks. "For them to be a family."

That's why she'd offered to let Tyler hold Charlotte. It's what Ainsley would have wanted, even if seeing the two of them together made Meg realize that in the blink of an eye, she'd become an outsider. *"She's his."*

Blood. Biology. No judge could deny that.

Russell moved quietly, going down on one knee to join her in front of the sofa. "Then why did Ainsley leave custody to you?"

Meg wasn't sure why she turned. Why she looked. Maybe because of the words. Maybe because of his voice, the gentle, reassuring warmth. *The intimacy.*

The reason didn't matter. She lifted her eyes to his, felt the zing of confusion all over again. "Because he wasn't here," she said. "Ainsley had big dreams, but she had no way of knowing if he'd be back."

The green of Russell's eyes flashed. "I wish it had been you that called me...not Lori."

She'd thought about it, but didn't see the point in starting to lean on someone who would soon be gone. "After the other night, I wasn't sure you were still here."

Russell put down the block he'd been fingering. "You really think I would leave without saying goodbye?"

Meg didn't know what she thought. She only knew that Charlotte's father had finally blown into town— and there was a very real chance she would be the one saying goodbye.

Throat tight, she twisted toward her niece. How would she do it? How would she ever find the strength to say goodbye?

"What if he wants her?" Just saying the words made her physically ill. "I can't do it," she whispered. "I can't lose her, too."

"Meggie—"

"She's all I have." One day she'd been living alone, a driven businesswoman. The next, she'd sat rocking a little girl who'd just lost her mother. And in the ensuing days and weeks, the impossible had happened. Charlotte had filled Meg's life with an amazing sense of purpose, all those nights spent holding her as she cried, rocking her, soothing her, promising...

The little laughs and big grins...

Joy. And discovery.

Mornings in the park and afternoons on the sofa, splashing in the bathtub and cuddling in the big bed.

Now the reality of Ainsley's soldier changed everything. No matter how badly Meg wished otherwise, no matter how badly she wanted to take Charlotte and flee, lose herself in the fantasy, she couldn't deny the truth.

"What if I stay?"

She looked up, found Russell watching her through completely unreadable eyes. She'd always hated his ability to do that. "What?"

"I'll tell the bureau I won't be there next week."

"Why?"

"So I can stay here," he said as Charlotte crawled toward him. He kept his eyes on Meg, but somehow at the same time invited the baby into his lap. "And help make sure that boy never takes Charlotte from you."

Meg blinked. For a moment she didn't think she'd

heard him right, but the way he kept looking at her told her that she had. "That boy is her father—and I'm not her mother."

"I'm her uncle," he said as Charlotte lifted a hand to the whiskers at his jaw and giggled.

The sight hurt. "But eventually you'll leave again, and then what happens?" Either way, Meg lost. "You can't take a child with you—"

"What if I didn't?"

The question stopped her cold.

"What if I stayed…this time for good?"

Everything in the cozy family room seemed amplified—the glare of the sun through the windows, the low buzz of silence, even the hard press of the wood floor. "I've asked myself that question a thousand times."

His eyes met hers. "So have I."

She stared at him—at them, man and child. Uncle and niece. "Did you come up with any answers?"

There, that was all it took. A sharp question straight to the point, and finally Russell looked away. It wasn't obvious, more like a slight shift in his attention from woman to child.

But Meg saw, and she had her answer.

Charlotte picked up a block and shoved it at her uncle, trying to feed it to him. Playfully he took it from her and pretended to nibble on the edges.

There was nothing playful about the way he sidestepped Meg's question. "Tyler is practically a kid himself. He's just back from Iraq, no job, unsettled. Unmarried."

Meg's heart started to pound really hard.

"What judge in his right mind would take an infant from a stable environment—"

"No." The word tore out of her as she automatically brought a hand to her mouth.

"I'm Ainsley's brother," he continued. "A blood relative."

And suddenly Meg knew, didn't need to hear another word. But he kept going, slowly, relentlessly, as if the past and the future were fused somehow—and children were interchangeable.

"As man and wife…"

CHAPTER TEN

Eleven months before

THE STRANGER EASED CLOSER, until there was no space between them. Then his hand dipped beneath the table, the warmth of his palm pressing against her thigh. "Maybe we should get out of here," he suggested. "Go somewhere where I can—" his eyes heated "—make you happy again."

Her throat burned. Her chest squeezed. From across the room, the song on the jukebox changed, but she barely noticed. There was only the steady advance of the hated numbness…and the man offering to chase it away.

"I'd like that," she said, lifting her hand to his face, wanting to touch—

"Leave her alone, you son of a bitch!" With those words another man emerged from the crowded dance floor, barreling toward them like some kind of avenging angel, and for a shattering breath, her heart surged.

Then she blinked against the haze and brought Trey into focus. He descended on the table and reached for Cody, yanked him by the arm. "What kind of lowlife are you?" he demanded. "Preying on a vulnerable woman…"

Cody drew himself to his full height, lifting his

hands as he did so. "Easy, brother," he drawled. "It's not like she was saying no."

"But I am." Lori's husband stared Cody down for a long heartbeat, until the confused stranger backed down, backed away. Then Trey turned toward her, reached for her. "Come on, darlin', let's go."

Meg stiffened. "What do you think you're doing?"

"Isn't that obvious?"

She wasn't sure she'd ever been more mortified in her life. "You have no right—"

"This isn't about rights," he said, pulling her to her feet. His hand found hers, and he all but dragged her through the pulse and throb of the music, into the warm spring night. "This is about friends," he muttered. "This is about making sure you don't throw away—"

She didn't want to hear any more. Reeling, she ripped from his arms and staggered back. "I don't need—"

Trey caught her before she fell. "Yes, you do," he said. "Ainsley's in labor."

Present Day

"As a man and wife, combined with the custodial papers Ainsley drew up, we would have a good chance of keeping Charlotte."

The words came at Meg like darts, each piercing deeper than the one before, penetrating layer after layer, slicing to the bone. Immediately she stood, took a step back. She wasn't sure why, but somehow that seemed important.

Russell stood, too, bringing Charlotte with him, her hand once again fiddling with his whiskers. It was like looking through the threads of time, to an alternate reality that had slipped by them.

Dreams weren't supposed to hurt. Dreams weren't supposed to shatter. But the promise was no longer there, and the smooth edges had turned sharp.

"You make it sound so simple," she said, careful to keep her voice neutral, neither shocked nor alarmed.

Russell kissed the top of Charlotte's head. "It can be."

"No." Meg took another step back as something dark and awful slipped through her. "It doesn't work like that," she said, trying to keep her breaths steady, normal. She'd moved past that. She'd moved forward, fixed herself. "We can't just pretend...."

This time it was Russell who stilled.

"Something broke," she tried again. But the spinning got faster, the past, the present, sucking at her, blurring. "After Hope died..."

She wasn't the same woman who'd once promised to love him forever. She wasn't the same woman who'd watched him drive away. The pieces had fallen everywhere. She'd made mistakes, done things she wasn't proud of. It had been months before she'd put things back together. Even now she wasn't sure she'd found them all.

"We can't go back," she said, scrambling to fill the silence between them, because he wasn't saying anything, just kept standing there with Charlotte in his arms looking at her as if he had no idea who she was. "I don't want to. I've moved on, and so have you. I love Charlotte with all my heart, Russell, but she doesn't change anything. She's not our daughter. We can't just plug her into the hole in our hearts and pretend the past two years never happened."

He winced, as if she'd physically slapped him. "Plug

her into the hole in our hearts? What the hell are you talking about?"

The alternative was worse. "You left, Russell." Three words. But for Meg, they summed up everything. "You walked away." From her, the promises they'd made, the forever he'd claimed to want. "You really think you can just come back now because Charlotte is here, and pick up where we left off? Play Mommy and Daddy as if the past two years never happened?" It was all she could do not to grab Charlotte from his arms. She deserved better. "That suddenly everything will be okay—that *we'll* be okay?"

"Goddamn it, Meg—"

"I want more than that." Only a few minutes before, she'd stepped back. Now she stepped toward him. "I want more than a marriage held together by duct tape and fear and legal maneuvers. I *deserve* more."

His lips almost seemed to curl. "Even if that means losing Charlotte?"

It was a low blow, and they both knew it. "You make it sound so black-and-white."

"It's called choices, Meg. That's what life is about— not just the ones we make, but the ones we don't make."

"Isn't that what we've been doing the past two years?" she asked, not furiously, but with surprising finesse. "Living with the choice you made?"

The lines of his face tightened, but for a long moment he said nothing, just looked from her to the credenza, where their wedding picture had once stood. All the while Charlotte kept right on squirming, moving on from his chin to play with his mouth. "I saw your mom today."

Meg wasn't sure what surprised her more—the words

themselves, or the utter quiet in his voice. Her husband and her mother had always adored each other. Sure, there'd been some in-law teasing, but the affection and respect had been obvious.

Lilah had been devastated when he left.

She'd been even more devastated as weeks rolled into months, and her insistence that he would come back never came true.

"She kicked my butt in video bowling," he said.

And despite everything, Meg couldn't help but laugh. "Yeah, she usually does."

Her mother had purchased the big TV and video system all on her own—and from what Meg could tell, Lilah and Ray spent hours honing their skills.

"She also held up a mirror for me to look in."

The laughter faded as quickly as it had arrived. "She does that, too."

Charlotte had moved on to his hair, running her fingers through the thick waves, mussing it, but Russell barely looked as if he noticed. His eyes were narrow, dark. He looked like a man who'd just taken a look behind a closed door, and wished that he hadn't.

"Regrets are poison, Meg. They kill you from the inside out."

She didn't need to be told that. "Is that what my mom said? Or personal experience?"

A harsh sound broke from his throat. "Maybe a little of both."

She swallowed hard.

"Tell me, Meggie…what will you regret more?" His voice was all quiet again. Deceptively so. "Taking a chance…or not taking one?"

Her heart started to pound. Everyone always touted honesty, but no one talked about what to do when everything was heaped out on the table. "Just go, Russell. Please."

A few nights before, when she'd come home to find him and Charlotte sleeping on the couch, she'd had to all but push him out the door. Now he didn't even hesitate.

It was as if he couldn't get out of there fast enough.

"You got it," he said, placing a giggling Charlotte back on the ground with her blocks. Then he straightened and looked Meg straight in the eye. "I'll go. Just remember…this time you asked."

"KEY-KEY-KEY," CHARLOTTE babbled into the phone, and, surveying long tables packed with auction items, Meg knew her niece was no doubt pawing all over one of her mother's cats. "Mama-mama."

The swell of warmth was immediate, and had absolutely nothing to do with the record high set that afternoon. Typical springtime in Texas, the temperature could—and did—bounce between record lows and highs in a matter of hours.

It was why they got such great storms.

Even now, clouds gathered against the western horizon.

"She's probably tired," Meg told her mom a few minutes later. In full multitask mode, she shifted a wooden picture frame decorated with a scattering of small, vintage crosses to a more prominent position on the narrow table. The artist, a friend of Ainsley's, had sweetly donated a few of her creations for the silent auction.

It was hard to believe that after all the months planning—and the whirlwind of the past two days—opening night of the festival was finally here.

"She didn't take a good nap today," she said, grateful her mother had volunteered to babysit. "You might want to try 'Hush Little Baby'…she likes that one."

"We'll be just fine," her mother said. "Now you just go on and enjoy yourself."

Meg intended to try.

"So have you heard from him since the other day?" Julia asked after Meg wound down the call.

"Not a word."

Beside her, Lori picked up a second frame, this one adorned with a hand-painted fleur-de-lys. "Which 'him'?"

Meg surveyed the crowd making its way along the long tables assembled for the auction. Locals and visitors alike literally streamed into the pavilion. "Neither." Two days had passed and not a word from Russell or Tyler. For all she knew, they'd both left town.

You really think I'd leave without saying goodbye?

She didn't know what to think anymore. Up until the week before, her thoughts had been clear and focused. She'd seen her future spread out before her, and she'd been going after it with renewed focus.

Now all the man she'd been in the process of divorcing had to do was walk into the same room as her and she could barely breathe.

What if I stay?

The question taunted.

What if he stayed?

The dream, the one she'd been so sure was dead and buried, whispered anew.

Around it, fear and caution wove a tight cocoon.

She'd yet to mention Russell's suggestion to anyone, not even her mother. She wasn't sure why.

"Try not to worry," Julia said as they passed a basket

of homemade jellies and jams. "There's no way Russell will let that boy take Charlotte from you."

Meg tensed. "It might not be up to Russell."

Lori's sharp intake of breath was immediate. "That's never going to happen," she promised. "No one's going to take that child from you."

Meg swallowed hard. She'd been back on her feet for close to a year, but the shame of how far she'd once fallen lingered. Bad decisions had consequences.

"Not while I have a breath in my body," she whispered.

Beyond where they stood in the tent, the makeshift midway came to life. To the left, food vendors and artisans lined Main Street. To the right...carnival rides.

"Thatta girl," Julia said. "Hey, let me know if you see Faith, okay? She promised she'd be here with the kids."

Meg crossed to the back row of auction items. "I didn't know they were back," she said. Julia's younger sister had gone on an extended trip several months before. Meg had begun to doubt she was coming back. Sometimes a change of venue helped.

Sometimes it didn't.

Farther down, she picked up a certificate entitling two lucky guests to an expense-paid weekend at the oldest bed-and-breakfast in Pecan Creek, the Magnolia Manor.

"Can you believe she's opening again?" Lori asked.

For over a year the place had been closed, following the death of its elderly owners in a suspicious fire. Now the Fieldings' granddaughter, Liz, was reopening the doors.

"Think the ghosts are included?" Meg asked. She

couldn't quite say she was a believer—she and Russell had never experienced anything that could not be explained—but there was no denying the litany of weird stories.

"Maybe you should ask Russell," Lori said.

The image formed before she could stop it, of Russell stretched out on one of the big antique beds. Chances were he was not staying in the same room where they'd first made love—and that particular bed had no doubt been tossed after the fire—but still. The image lingered.

"You gonna bid?" Lori asked.

In answer, Meg returned the certificate to the table and moved on. Next to Uncle Ralph's auction entry was the *Gazette*'s, a complimentary six-month subscription.

So far there were no bids.

"Is Trey around?" Meg asked.

"Somewhere," Lori said. "They were out pretty late last night."

"Who was?"

"The guys," Lori said, upping Meg's Uncle Ralph's bid. "Trey and Lance and…"

Meg looked up.

"Poker," Lori explained, and with the word came the memory: Boys' Poker Night…Girls' Spa Day.

It seemed like a lifetime before. "Well, I guess that means we should—" Meg started, but stopped when she realized Julia was no longer with them. She looked around, turning abruptly and running straight into a woman wearing a long trench coat.

"Excuse me—" Meg's mouth dropped open as she took in the woman's large out-of-style white sunglasses and the turquoise scarf wrapped around her head. *"Julia?"*

"Shh!" Her friend closed in on her, leaning in as she spoke. "Don't say my name."

Lori worked hard not to laugh.

"Um…okay," Meg said. "But…you want to tell me what's going on?"

Incognito, Julia ushered them past the remaining auction items to the end of the table, where no one else stood. *"He's here."*

Meg started to look around, but Julia stopped her. "Not now. I don't want him to know we're talking about him."

"Talking about…who?" For the faintest of moments, Meg had thought she meant Russell. But no way would Julia be acting like this over Russell.

"The witch doctor." Julia's voice held equal parts ridicule—and excitement.

"Noah Blackstone," Lori supplied, in case Meg hadn't figured it out on her own. Which she had. "From the Brookhaven Institute."

The new sleep disorder research facility just east of town, the one Julia insisted was cloaked in secrecy. Granted, the place was surrounded by an electric fence, and the only entrance was via a manned guard shack.

But heightened security did not necessarily equate shady business.

"How do you know it's him?" As far as Meg knew, Blackstone had not yet ventured into town. It was a sore spot with the locals, who'd been told the new institute would bring a steady stream of dollars to Pecan Creek.

"Because she's obsessed with him," Lori said. "Ever notice how often she's got Google pulled up?"

"Not *him*," Julia said in a fierce whisper. "With what he's *doing* out there."

Construction had started over two years before. Local crews had bid for jobs, but the electricians, plumbers— even general craftsmen who'd wanted to install Sheet-rock or paint the walls—had all been turned down.

"Just look at him," Julia all but purred. "He's got it written all over his face."

"You mean I can look now?" Meg teased, turning to follow the direction of Julia's stare. Through the grow-ing crowd and dimming light, she found lots of familiar faces, including her cousin Faith. She needed to go say hi.

"By the back entrance," Julia said. "On his cell phone."

Meg saw him then, the dark-haired man dressed all in black, standing off by himself. Definitely a stranger. Tall, olive-skinned...Native American maybe, based upon the prominence of his cheekbones and the deep set of his eyes.

"What exactly is all over his face?" Meg asked. "Other than whiskers..."

"Secrets," Julia said. "Lies."

Trying to be patient, Meg turned back to her friend. "Julia. Please. You've been watching way too much TV."

The scarf and sunglasses left little of Julia's face visible. "Just one month," she said. "Just give me one month, and I promise I'll put the *Gazette* on the map."

Meg didn't know whether to laugh...or groan. So for the time being, she punted. "We'll talk Monday." She had no reason to believe anything shady or contro-versial was happening at the Brookhaven Institute, but something told her Julia needed this. Her cousin was restless, craving…something. Anything. She and Lance had married so young. Meg wasn't sure they even talked anymore.

Too well, Meg knew what a recipe for disaster that was.

"I'm going to want details," she said. "A plan…what you're going to do and what you hope to find."

Julia's mouth widened into a smile Meg hadn't seen in ages. "You're the best," she said, moving in for a hug, but stopping at the last minute. "He's on the move," she said.

And then Julia, too, was on the move, slipping along the back of the tent, toward the spot Noah Blackstone had last stood.

Meg looked at Lori. "Well, then," she said, heading back toward the last table. She had less than an hour before the first round of auction winners was announced. "Why don't we…"

The picture stopped her cold. It was a recent one, from just a few days before, actually. In the field of bluebonnets. After Charlotte had started crying again, Ray had lifted her in his arms, leaving Meg sitting surrounded by bluebonnets and red poppies. She'd drawn her knees to her chest, smiling as she watched the baby play with Ray's glasses. He must have snapped the picture then, capturing just that moment, the smile that came from somewhere so deep inside.

Now that picture was framed; next to it sat a sign: Spend The Evening With The Publisher Of The *Piney Woods Gazette!*

"Don't be mad!" Lori gushed.

Meg spun toward her…friend. "You did this?"

Lori's grin took the edge off Meg's surprise. "And

Julia," Lori said. "We thought…well, it's for a good cause."

Warily, Meg looked back at the form, just as Lori let out a low whistle. "Look at the size of that number!"

Meg did. It was high. *Very* high.

"Someone wants you bad," Lori said, playing all innocent when Meg quickly looked up. "I mean an evening with you…to support the March of Dimes, of course."

But Meg was already scanning the tent, wondering who.

THE LAST OF THE SUN slipped beneath the horizon, leaving an otherworldly glow. Reds and oranges and pinks swirled against the growing darkness, hinting at what the meteorologists had talked about earlier in the day, a cold front sweeping toward East Texas.

The question wasn't if it would rain. But when…and how much.

Russell couldn't remember a Wildflower Festival without rain. He and Meg had once joked that the festival should be moved out of thunderstorm season, but thunderstorms and wildflowers went together like whiskey and cold nights.

Lifting his camera, he adjusted the aperture before capturing the angry western sky.

"Good crowd," Trey commented, juggling a corn dog in one hand and a bag of kettle corn in the other. "Last year between the winter drought and cold April, it was a complete bust."

Lowering his camera, Russell flagged down a beer vendor. "Two Sam Adams—" he started, but Trey shook his head. "One, then," Russell said.

Trey had stuck to water the night before, too. That was new.

But so much else was the same. With each step Russell took, familiarity rushed back, as if not a day had passed since he'd last walked Main Street. Sure there were people he didn't recognize, but it had always been like that. Pecan Creek was a small town, but not *that* small.

But still…he kept his eye out for Tyler.

"Russell?"

He turned as a thin blond woman rushed out of the ice-cream shop with two young kids on either side of her.

"Omigosh!" she said, as recognition brightened her face. "It *is* you!"

"Faith," he said, opening his arms to Meg's cousin. He hugged her hard, stunned by how much weight she'd lost. She'd never been a big woman, nor had she been rail thin like this. She'd been curvy.

Now she was bony.

"I didn't know you were back," she said, pulling away to smile up at him. "Hannah? Ryan?" The kids flanked her, each busy with a double-scoop waffle cone. "Do you remember Uncle Rusty?"

He wasn't technically their uncle, but he'd learned people in the South tended to attach the term to almost anyone in their inner circle, family or not.

The little girl, a miniature replica of her mother, shook her head, sending blond pigtails bobbing. Two years ago she'd been…four, Russell thought. That made her six now.

Ryan—who had to be twelve and could not have looked more like his father, Todd, if he were a clone—nodded. "Yeah."

"How long are you here?" Faith asked. "Where are you staying? I haven't talked to Meg in forever!"

"The Manor," Russell answered before the conversation veered in an unwanted direction. With only a few more days until his Monday-afternoon flight, he'd spent most of the day finishing up at Ainsley's house. He'd also talked to his lawyer.

"The Manor?" Faith's eyes widened. "Wow, how's that working out for you?"

Trey cleared his throat, looked away. He'd been there the night before, along with Lance. They'd been in the room Liz's family called the parlor. They'd been playing poker when the scent of pipe tobacco filtered into the room—and a decanter of whiskey fell from the shelf.

Parlor tricks, they'd all decided with a good laugh. Liz was no doubt gearing up for her grand opening.

"Sleeping with my eyes open," Russell joked, not too worried about anyone else's ghosts. "Other than that, so far, so good."

"Then you weren't really sleeping." With suspicion in his voice, Ryan narrowed his eyes. "I heard in the middle of the night, like when everyone is sleeping, sometimes you can hear real footsteps down the hall."

"I'll let you know," Russell said with a conspiratorial wink. "So where's your dad?" he asked, looking beyond the trio. He'd always liked Todd, had even helped coach a Little League team with him, despite the fact Russell had grown up playing soccer. "Is he around?"

The change happened so fast it stopped Russell cold. All the animation drained from Ryan's face. He froze, his eyes going hard. Hannah's eyes filled. And before Faith could speak, Russell knew he wasn't going to like what she had to say.

"He's...*gone.*"

Faith's voice was so soft Russell barely made out her words. Around them the festival breezed on, families sweeping by, a trio going into the ice-cream shop, a young man with a very pregnant young wife sitting on a nearby bench, four boys running ahead of a harried mom, a father with a little girl on his shoulders. And with the distorted strains of live country-and-western music from the gazebo across the street, the pieces fell together, and Russell realized why Faith looked so fragile.

"Christ, I'm sorry," he said, hating the helplessness, the realization of just how much had changed since he'd been gone. Never in a million years could he have imagined a man like Todd walking out on his family. "I didn't know. I—"

"It's been a year," Faith said, her smile sad but somehow brave at the same time. "It's been tough."

"I'm sure," Russell said. "Look, if there's anything I can do..."

"I'm sorry about Ainsley," Faith said in an oddly wistful voice. "She was so good to us in those first few weeks after the funeral. She was as pregnant as she could be, but that didn't stop her from taking Hannah to the park day after day."

Faith kept talking, but one word drowned out all those that came after it.

Funeral.

Todd Redington hadn't walked out on his family. At least not on purpose. The high school football coach only a year or two younger than Russell had died.

Everything inside Russell went cold. His chest felt as though it had a rope around it. His throat, hands. Why hadn't Ainsley told him?

"…so sorry she's gone…"

He made out those words, forced himself to move, pulling Meg's cousin into his arms, this time more gently than before. A widow at thirty. Sometimes life could be so goddamn unfair.

After a long moment he pulled back and put his hands to her face, slid the hair back from her cheeks and looked into brown eyes brimming with devastation— and resilience. "I wish I'd been here."

Her smile was tight. "Thank you," she whispered. "You were missed."

Automatically he glanced toward the auction tent.

"She needed you," Faith said, lifting her eyes to his as he turned back to her. "So, so badly."

"Mom—" Hannah tugged on Faith's arm. "When are we gonna go?"

"It wasn't until I lost Todd that I realized what it had been like for her. Except Todd didn't have a choice. I just couldn't help but think if you'd been here…" Faith's voice trailed off as Trey turned back toward them. Their eyes met. Something silent flashed between them.

Russell didn't need to be a trained journalist to see the unspoken. It had been happening repeatedly since he returned to Pecan Creek.

"If I'd been here…what?" he asked.

But Faith just shook her head. "This time are you going to stay?"

CHAPTER ELEVEN

THE QUESTION WAS A SIMPLE one, obvious even, but the edge to Faith's tone made it sound more like an indictment.

"Get to know your niece," she added.

Russell stepped back, not sure why he hadn't realized how hard coming home would be.

Home.

The word stung.

"Mom," little Hannah said again, with a hard tug to her mother's purse. Faith finally looked down at the little girl.

"Didn't mean to keep you," Russell said by way of extracting himself. Faith glanced up and flashed him a tight smile, reminding him so much of her cousin as she'd been that last night when he'd left for Africa. At the time he'd thought Meg cold, unfeeling.

Now, with Faith, the realization that she felt far more than she wanted anyone to see pierced him in a way he didn't understand.

"What the hell happened?" he asked a few minutes later as he and Trey made their way toward the growing crowd at the auction tent.

His friend finished off a bottle of water and tossed it in a nearby recycle can. "One of those fluke things... thought it was just the flu."

Russell stepped around a group of lanky teens with

those stupid baggy jeans down around their asses and headed toward the front door of the tent.

"Turned into pneumonia," Trey said. "There was some underlying infection. Took him fast."

Russell frowned. Faith was such a sweetheart. Like Julia and Lance, she and Todd had been together since high school.

"There you are," Lori said, materializing from the back of the tent. She swept in and pressed up for a quick kiss, running her hand from Trey's forehead to his cheek as she did so. "Everything okay?"

He slid an arm around his wife and anchored her to his side. "You tell me," he said. "Do we have any money left?"

She grinned. "We'll know soon enough." Then to Russell, "Pretty impressive, isn't it?"

It was. He looked around the huge tent, with its six long tables of auction items, the proceeds benefiting the March of Dimes. From what he could tell, almost every item had at least one bid.

"She worked her tail off," Lori said, gesturing toward the temporary stage, where Meg spoke with two older women he recognized but could no longer name. "She made it happen."

The ping of pride surprised him. He watched her, the warmth of her smile and the excitement in her eyes, the way her hair fell against her shoulders as she moved effortlessly, laughing and shaking hands. Dressed in cargo capris and a simple feminine-cut T-shirt in melon, she looked so much like the girl she'd been all those years ago, when he'd first come to Pecan Creek, before heartbreak had stripped away that sense of vitality that had always made Meg…Meg.

"Now, if she can just save the paper," Lori muttered,

but as Russell turned back toward her, his gaze snagged on a picture instead. Meg sat surrounded by bluebonnets and poppies, knees to her chest, her smile radiant. But it was the auction form that stopped him...

Amount: $10,000
Bidder: Anonymous

"Pretty impressive," Lori said as Trey let out a low whistle. "So when are you going to tell her about the bid?"

Russell looked up, watched Meg move toward the podium. "There's nothing to tell." He'd always known time moved forward. He knew life went on. But standing there watching Meg reach for the microphone and knowing some son of a bitch would soon step forward to claim his evening with the editor of the *Piney Woods Gazette,* Russell wanted to grab the stupid form and rip it to shreds. Meg was a young, healthy woman, alone in that big house night after night....

His whole body tightened. Two years was a damn long time. He knew that. He'd lived it. But he'd been in the field, on assignment. He'd lost himself in his work.

What had Meg lost herself in?

Who?

Who'd been there to keep her company? To keep her warm?

Who'd been there to comfort her when she cried...?

Something inside him started to boil. It was slow and insidious, just like the images. He'd never imagined *her* life going on, goddamn it. When he'd thought of her, it had always been as his wife.

The one who'd shut him out.

Now as he watched her greet the crowd, this beautiful, confident woman who'd pieced her life back together and moved on—*who'd told him explicitly and repeatedly that she did not want him here*—something dark and possessive twisted through him.

Not able to just stand there one second longer, he turned from the sight of her and cut his way through the crowd.

SHE COULDN'T SEE HIM. He'd been there, with Lori and Trey, scowling up at the stage with a ferocity that had made her blood hum, even as it unsettled her. Then she'd turned to say hello to someone, and when she'd looked back out toward the tent, he'd been gone. But she'd swear she could feel him still, somewhere. *Watching.*

Uncharacteristically edgy, Meg worked her way through the stack of auction forms, reading off the description of each item and the winning bid, smiling as each bidder came forward. All the while she scanned the crowd, looking.

For a ridiculous, fleeting moment there, when she'd seen Russell with Lori and Trey—and the embarrassing auction photo and evening she had *so* not authorized— her heart had kicked hard against her ribs, and deep inside, she'd started to wonder. What if he did stay? What if she said yes? What if they gave it a try...raising Charlotte?

What if they were a family?

He'd made it sound so easy.

Fear, she knew. It was fear that had led her to say no. Fear that made her protect herself, when a vast part of her just wanted to trust—and try again.

But now the crowd waited for the next auction item, and Russell was nowhere in sight.

"Okay, folks, looks like we've got some adventurous souls among us," she said with a breeziness she didn't really feel, "if you'll excuse the pun, that is."

Lori and Trey stood toward the front, but Julia was nowhere to be seen. Neither was Lance—or Noah Blackstone.

"We've all heard the stories," she said. "We all know the history. It's been almost two years since we lost our beloved Magnolia Manor to fire and foreclosure, but Rita Mae and Hank's granddaughter has managed to resurrect the family's legacy, and the Magnolia Manor is again ready to tempt those who enjoy tempting fate."

Her quick twinge of unease surprised her. Sure Russell was staying there—the only guest at the moment. And sure Liz was several years younger, a complete knockout and, with absolutely no baggage, a definite temptress of fate.

But when was the last time Meg had felt...jealous?

"With a bid of twenty-five hundred dollars, our winner of a weekend for two at the Magnolia Manor is...bidder 100423A."

A shriek rose from the back of the crowd as a young couple Meg had never seen made their way to the front of the tent. She shook their hands and directed them to the far side of the platform, where Uncle Ralph's wife, Ruby, was taking care of formalities.

Meg worked through the rest of the auction items, before reaching the last sheet of paper...the one she'd been avoiding for over half an hour. The picture stared up at her, the smile Ray had captured without her knowing it. Only minutes before he'd snapped the picture, she'd stood with Russell, had looked into the green of his eyes for the first time in almost two years.

She should not have been smiling.

But against the sterile auction form, the warm, visceral glow could not be denied.

Nor could the breathtakingly high bid. There were three entries on the form, the third and final so ridiculously high it was as if someone had staked their claim and scared everyone else off.

She looked up abruptly and saw him just inside the entrance, arms crossed, eyes narrowed and focused exclusively on her. A good fifty yards separated them, but she would have sworn she could feel him.

Everything else kind of blurred. She knew she had to say something, that everyone was watching her, waiting, but when she opened her mouth, the cottony feeling forced her to clear her throat.

The rush of warmth crept up her neck and burned her cheeks, made her want to step back from the spotlight, so no one else would see. No one else would know.

But that was a lie and she knew it. It wasn't the crowd of friends and strangers that made her want to step back. It wasn't them she cared about seeing...noticing. *Knowing.*

It was him. It was Russell. He just stood there, his dark shirt and faded jeans not so different from the other men's, but the very stillness of him set him apart.

In sync with the storm outside, her heart thrummed hard and low and deep. He'd done that in class sometimes, walked into the buzzing lecture hall and taken his place at the lecturn, standing absolutely still until silence fell, waiting with excruciating patience until he was in full command of the moment.

Of her.

Sometimes he'd done the same thing in bed.

The thought shook her.

She couldn't remember the last time they'd been in bed, that she'd reached for him. She remembered him reaching for her, time and time again. Just as she remembered turning away from him, time and time again.

She just couldn't remember the last time. There'd been no drop of a gavel. No pause or pronouncement. No indication, no way of knowing that this touch would be the last.

The spotlight glared hotter, bringing dampness to the back of her neck. Woodenly she reached for the glass of punch a volunteer had brought over as Lori started to move. Maybe that's what broke the moment. Or maybe it was the baby in the front row, in her mother's arms, starting to cry. Or the older man coughing toward the back of the tent. Or the blur of movement to the side, almost like a woman running. In some vague corner of her mind Meg would have sworn she saw the flash of a trench coat.

But the moment broke as Lori arrived with a bright smile and laughter in her voice.

"Quit being so modest," she teased, rushing to the rescue with the easy grace that was all her own. She swept onto the stage and took her place by Meg, reaching for the last sheet of paper. "We all know what you saved for last." Grinning, she angled the microphone a little lower. "Just like we all know you don't want to brag."

Meg swallowed against the dryness of her throat, but could not stop looking toward the back of the tent, where Russell still stood, isolated somehow, despite the three or four hundred people crowded around him.

"We have one last auction item," Lori said with a breeziness Meg had not heard from her friend in a long time. "And that item is—" her smile widened "—our very own Meg."

Laughter erupted.

Russell didn't move, didn't smile. Didn't laugh.

"We did this without her knowledge," Lori added, "and, like everything else this evening, to honor her favorite charity, the March of Dimes. One evening with our favorite newspaper owner…" With great drama she let out a sharp whistle as she lifted the auction form to the crowd. "Can you say *twelve…thousand… dollars?*"

This time, it was applause from the entire crowd that thundered through the tent. Except for Russell. Who still didn't move. Still just watched.

He almost looked…angry.

The urge to back away gripped Meg, but she made herself stand still, grateful that it was Lori who took the brunt of the spotlight.

"Will the winner," she called, "100479A—" she paused, hesitated, looked to the back of the tent, directly at Russell, "—please come forward."

Silence fell as everyone glanced around. And though she hated herself for it, Meg's eyes found Russell, and the rhythm of her pulse echoed so hard in her blood it felt like a hammer in her temples, in every other pulse point of her body.

But Russell didn't move. Didn't step forward—didn't look around.

And then the gasp came from the right side of the tent, as the crowd jostled around to let a lone figure move forward. A man Meg had seen an hour or so

before, when Julia had breathlessly begged her friends
not to blow her cover.

Noah Blackstone.

AROUND MEG, THE CROWD drained from the pavilion,
commotion giving way to silence. Here and there folks
lingered, friends chatting, parents tending to children,
several teens busily texting, several more all wrapped
up in one another.

But Russell was gone.

He'd walked out within seconds of Noah Blackstone
stepping onto the platform. One moment Russell had
been there, watching her through eyes harder than steel,
as if she'd betrayed him somehow. Then he was just…
gone.

After all this time, his ability to walk so quickly and
easily away shouldn't still hurt.

Even now, over fifteen minutes later, the urge to go
after him lingered.

"Thirsty?"

Meg forced a smile as she looked up at the man
who'd shelled out an inordinate sum of money to spend
the evening with her.

She was so going to kill someone, probably Julia,
who remained conspicuously absent.

"Yes, thank you," she said, accepting another glass
of punch. After more than an hour of nonstop talking,
her throat *was* dry. She took a deep sip as she scrambled
for something witty or intelligent to say—but came up
blank. She'd never been a prize before. She'd never been
bought and paid for.

Noah Blackstone was hardly a talker, either. He was
taller than she'd first realized, well over six feet. She
had to tilt her head to see his face, making it impossible

to study him without being obvious. Definitely Native American. The wide, sharp cheekbones were a dead giveaway. And his eyes were as dark as his hair, deep set and…knowing. That was the first word that came to mind. The man looked as if he knew things.

Five minutes in his company, and Julia's cover would be complete toast. They'd yet to share more than a few casual words, but already Meg knew her cousin would never get away with scamming this man. There was a vibration to him, she realized. Weird word, but she couldn't shake the low buzz he seemed to emit.

"You, my friend, look tired," he said, his voice neither warm nor seductive like Russell's, but still rich, low, commanding in a way that made you want to hear what he had to say.

"And I suppose you have just the cure for that," she quipped before she could stop herself. The warm flush was instinctive—rarely was Meg so forward or crass with someone, especially a stranger.

The renowned researcher's mouth—hard and unyielding moments before—twitched. "And if I said yes?"

Her eyes met his, and for the first time since this whole auction nightmare began, she smiled. "Then I'd say no."

Julia's target laughed. "Well, what do you know? An honest woman—and a journalist at that. I like that."

Then he was going to *love* Julia.

Meg glanced away, discarding the ridiculous thought as quickly as it formed. If this man and Julia tangled, there would be serious hell to pay.

"I've always been a big fan of sleep myself," she said. "Eight hours and I'm golden."

"When was the last time that happened?"

She blinked. "Pardon?"

"Eight hours," Blackstone said. "When was the last time you got eight uninterrupted hours of sleep?"

The question slipped in like a low blow. "Do I look that bad?" she tossed back, even as her mind spun for an answer. Not for him, but for her. How long had it been since she'd slept…really slept? Before Ainsley died and Charlotte came to live with her, there'd been little sleep, always work to do or some project, or…

She hated the *or*.

Even before Russell had left, before their baby died. Back before she was pregnant, before their desire to start a family had turned into a nightmare of medical tests and procedures…way back to those early days of their marriage, when they'd crawled into bed and made love, fallen asleep naked in each other's arms…

"That long?"

She glanced up, unnerved by the *knowing* in Blackstone's eyes. It was sharper than before, a needle ready to pierce.

"So is that why you placed the bid?" she asked. "To find out how much sleep I'm getting?"

His eyes narrowed. "No."

"Or maybe you'd like to know about my dreams," she suggested. She'd heard he was into that, too…or at least, that his clinic was. Dream therapy, Julia had called it.

"Only if you want to tell me."

When you dream…what do you see?

You really want me to answer that?

Deep inside, something shifted. She didn't want to think of Russell like that, alone in his bed at night. And she sure didn't want to think about what he saw when he closed his eyes—or why.

You. I see you.

Blinking, she looked up—and saw him. On the far right side of the tent, beside the drink station. Like before, he stood alone. And like before, his face was hard, unreadable.

And like before, the quickening was immediate.

"Megan?"

She took a deliberate sip of punch, concentrating on the tart sweetness as it slid down the back of her dry throat.

"Sometimes waking dreams—"

"It's Meg," she said, cutting off his psychobabble before she actually started to listen.

"Then Meg it is." He took the empty cup from her and tossed it toward the trash. "Let's get out of here."

A thousand excuses barged in from the growing silence around them, but Meg shooed them away. Despite the way Russell watched her, she had nothing to feel guilty about. This man had just forked out twelve thousand dollars to the March of Dimes on her behalf. No matter how unsettling she found him, she could give him a little more time.

Outside, the wind gusted stronger than she'd realized while inside the pavilion. Off to the west the sky flickered. They had a little longer before the storm swept in, but not much. With luck, it wouldn't be a repeat of the disaster from five years before, when softball-size hail had sent everyone running—and destroyed more than a few of the artisans' tents.

"Hungry?" Blackstone asked.

She glanced toward the vendors, where Lori and Trey waited in the smoothie line. "No, thanks." She continued to survey the crowd, in search of her cousin Faith. She couldn't imagine how hard it was to be back—

The thought stopped her.

Faith was back after only six months or so.

Russell was back after almost two years. So much had changed, but until that moment, she'd never stopped to wonder what it was like for him, returning to the town he'd abandoned to find that life had simply... moved on.

What if I stayed?

Not ready to go down that path, she twisted toward Noah Blackstone. "But you know what I *would* love?"

He almost smiled—almost. "You mean besides sleep?"

She surprised herself by grinning. "The Ferris wheel."

That definitely caught him off guard. But he recovered quickly and took her by the arm, steering her toward the midway. "The Ferris wheel it is, then."

The median age of the crowd plummeted as they passed the carousel and kiddie rides, the Fun House and Giant Slide, the Haunted House that had been malfunctioning as recently as late afternoon. Based on the length of the line, the problem had obviously been corrected.

"How long before you shut everything down?" Blackstone asked as thunder rumbled much closer.

"We've got a command center," she said as they joined the line for the Ferris wheel. "A meteorologist is on duty at all times, monitoring the radar and ham radio operators, the National Weather Service. As soon as a storm becomes imminent, we make the call."

Their process had become considerably more cautious after the injuries a few years before.

"So you never told me," Meg said as the line inched forward. "Why the big bid?"

His eyes seemed to gleam. "Maybe I'm just a man who appreciates a good cause."

The wince was automatic, even though she knew he meant the March of Dimes and not her. "Maybe."

They stepped forward as a few cages emptied. "Or maybe I'm just hedging my bets."

"What bets?"

"A beautiful woman—"

"Who just happens to run the local newspaper," she finished for him.

His lips twitched. "There is that," he said as the family in front of them stepped into a cage. "It's never a bad idea—"

"*Never* is a strong word."

Meg stiffened at the deceptively quiet voice, her body going achingly still as Russell materialized from behind her. The stillness from before still clung to him, but the edges were sharper, and for some insane reason, they thrilled her.

"So it is," Blackstone said as the attendant motioned for them to step forward. "So maybe I'll just start with tonight."

Russell stepped closer, positioning his body between hers and Blackstone's. "Or maybe not."

An odd little panic fluttered through Meg. At least, she thought it was panic. "Russell, you can't just—"

"Watch me," he said, reaching for her hand.

"Look," Blackstone said. "I don't know who you think you are, but—"

"Her husband."

Two words. That was all Russell said. But like a punch they stopped Noah Blackstone dead in his tracks.

The man Julia was convinced had some dark secret stilled, his gaze shifting from Meg to Russell, back to Meg.

"Very well, then," he said, stepping back as Russell led Meg past the gawking attendant to the waiting cage.

The second they were inside, she snatched back her hand. "Mind telling me what that was all about?" she asked as the attendant instructed them to buckle in.

As if nothing had just happened, Russell strapped in across from her. "I didn't like the way he was looking at you."

"Ma'am—" the pimply faced attendant called.

Meg sat down and grabbed for the belt. "You didn't like the way he was looking at me?"

"Like he was hungry," Russell said as the Ferris wheel started to revolve, "and you were a piece of prime rib."

To the west, lightning brightened the sky, followed seconds later by the roll of thunder.

"Won't be much longer," Russell commented with infuriating nonchalance.

Meg just sat there. And stared at him. The cage swung with the breeze as the ride lifted them into the night sky, pausing every few minutes to swap riders.

She wanted to be mad. She wanted to be furious. But as she looked at him while their little car rocked and swayed, something dark and drugging throbbed through her.

"You know who that was, don't you?" she asked.

Russell shrugged. "I do."

"Then you also know that he runs the research institute just west of town."

Again, another shrug. "I'm familiar."

"And I'm a reporter—" she started.

But he did not let her finish. "I saw Faith."

That got her. That stopped her. "Oh."

"She told me about Todd."

Instinctively Meg closed her eyes, hated what she saw there in the darkness of memory.

CHAPTER TWELVE

"IT WAS HORRIBLE," MEG SAID. "We just thought he had a cold, and then all of a sudden Julia is at my door in the middle of the night, telling me to get dressed...."

More lightning. More thunder. But Russell barely noticed.

"We were all there at the hospital," Meg was saying, "just standing there, unable to do anything, to believe that it was really happening, that Todd could really catch a cold and lapse into a coma."

And he hated the image that formed, of his friends and family gathered in some sterile waiting room—without him. "I wish I'd known."

"I...I tried to call you."

The words were quiet, barely audible over the rush of the wind. It was stronger up here, sending the little cage swaying like a flimsy leaf. Down below the festival whirred on, a blur of lights and music and beer and grease. But dangling like charms from a bracelet high off the ground, there was just Russell and Meg, and an honesty that rocked him. "When?"

Pain darkened her eyes. "The night he died. It was late when I got home and I couldn't sleep, didn't know what to do. Couldn't believe that he was just...gone. And I just kept thinking that you should have been there. That you needed to know."

He waited for her to finish. He watched the shadows

play across the paleness of her face, and wished like hell he could chase them away.

"I wanted…"

This time he moved. This time he couldn't just sit there and wait, not when need twisted him up inside. He yanked open his seat belt and slipped across the cage, not giving a damn how many rules he was breaking.

"What?" he asked, sliding in beside her. The seat was narrow. It was impossible to sit without touching.

He didn't even try.

He was so goddamn tired of playing by everyone else's rules.

"What did you want?"

Her eyes met his. They were dark, drenched with a devastation that reached inside, and punched. The word *want* glowed there, in the intimate blue of her gaze, even if she couldn't give it voice.

Him. She'd wanted him.

"You," she whispered. "I wanted you to know."

He wasn't sure what surprised him more. Her answer, or that she'd given him one. "Why?"

She blinked. "What?"

"Why did you want me to know?"

For a moment she seemed confused, as if she wasn't sure of the answer herself. Then she said, "Because you were part of us, I think. Because Todd always asked about you. Because…"

She started to look away, but he put a finger to her chin and urged her back. "Not this time," he said quietly. *"Not this time."*

Lightning lit up the sky. "I don't like thinking about that time." Thunder boomed—and the storm-warning bullhorn started to sound. "I wasn't used to being on my own then," she added. "You were gone, but when something bad happened, my instinct was still to reach for you."

The rare honesty, the image it invoked, twisted him up in ways he'd never expected. His wife had stopped reaching for him a long time ago. "Why didn't you leave a message?"

Another gust of wind tore through the Ferris wheel, as down below, the crowd started to scramble.

"I don't know," she whispered. "I…didn't know what to say."

Once, the nonanswer would have frustrated him. But the vulnerability in her eyes got to him, and he knew that for one of the first times in years, she was telling him the absolute, honest-to-God truth.

He wasn't sure he'd ever wanted—

God, he didn't know what he wanted.

To touch her again. To hold her. To crush her in his arms and make the chill go away. To stop the goddamn storm.

For her to reach for him…

The Ferris wheel moved faster, the car swinging erratically as the operator worked to get everyone off. Down below, other rides emptied as the street filled with a crowd jostling to leave.

I…didn't know what to say.

He didn't, either. That had been a major part of the problem. He'd tried. He'd tried so bloody hard to reach her. Be there for her. But after having the door repeatedly shut in his face, eventually he'd quit trying. He'd been so wrapped up in his own anger, so driven by the sting of rejection, that he'd insulated himself from seeing or feeling anything beyond what he wanted to see. Wanted to feel.

The anger had been easier. Rejection he could sink his teeth into. But guilt and helplessness…

They ate him alive.

Because he saw now. He felt. Sitting thigh to thigh in the cramped Ferris wheel cage, she didn't turn from him. She didn't hide. And finally he could see beyond the cool, untouchable facade she'd vanished behind after they lost their baby, the one she'd wrapped herself in. Lost herself in. He could see the woman he'd promised to love forever. Without hesitation she'd put her trust in him, given him her heart, to have and to hold, through good times and bad. But in the end he'd walked away, leaving her to walk alone. To hurt alone.

To suffer alone.

His wife.

"I'm sorry." The words tore from his throat, raw… ragged. And when her eyes met his and he saw the glow of confusion, of surprise, something dark and primitive slammed up against the walls and barriers that had taken over their marriage. Hurt, pride, ego, broken promises…they'd piled up like a crude dam between them, making it impossible to see anything else. To feel anything else. But now all he saw was Meggie, the trusting girl she'd been, the gutsy woman she'd become, the bravery and loyalty, the grit and determination, the longing.

It was the longing that got him. The longing that had him reaching for her, touching. Her body was soft, warm despite the tremor he felt rip through her. Instinct had him pulling her closer, fisting his hand in her hair as something inside him, too, started to shake.

She didn't push him away. She didn't shove at him, turn from him. Reject him. For the first time in two years she relaxed into him, rested against him. Let him...*be there*.

Damn it, it was all he'd ever wanted. To be there. To give. To heal.

When he'd first come back to Pecan Creek, it had been like walking into the past. But now he saw how ruthlessly life had marched forward. There'd been births and deaths. The paper was in trouble. The Manor had burned, closed, was about to be reopened. Lori and Trey were no longer carefree. Julia and Lance no longer looked at each other. And Meg...

She'd walked alone, but she'd walked strong. She'd weathered. And she'd endured.

But at what cost? some nasty voice inside whispered. At what cost?

"Meggie," he murmured into the first few splatters of rain, but then the car stopped moving and the attendant was there, yanking open the door and staring in at them.

"Hurry up," the kid said as reality came pouring back in. "Storm's a monster. I gotta get everyone off."

Meg jerked back, her gaze clear and alert as she looked around. "We have to make sure everyone finds cover!"

But Russell was already on his feet, reaching for her hand and helping her off the ride. As committee chair, she clearly felt a sense of responsibility.

"I'm sure everything is fine," he said, hurrying with her through the masses running toward the parking lots. The crowd had thinned considerably—East Texans did not take storms lightly. In addition to strong winds, rain and hail, tornadoes were a constant threat. Everyone remembered the F-5 that literally wiped a neighboring town from the map.

He remembered the way Meg had gone from shaken to strong-as-nails when they'd gone in search of a story for the paper, and ended up manning a Red Cross station instead.

"We have an evacuation process," she said as they ran against the push of the wind. "Shop owners are to open their doors. The mayor will open City Hall. Everyone should know—"

And apparently everyone did. "Well, how about that," Russell said as they rounded onto Main Street. Less than twenty minutes before, long lines had snaked around food vendors, with heavy crowds milling in and out of the big artisan pavilion.

Now tents flapped and trash swirled, but the main drag looked more like a ghost town. Only a few stragglers remained, a couple of vendors, some kids—and just about the entire Pecan Creek police force. They made their way up and down the street with flashlights and whistles, making sure everyone was out of the path of the increasingly violent wind.

"Come on," Russell called, as big raindrops and small pellets of hail dropped like bullets. "Let's get out of here." Tightening his hold on her hand, he urged her toward the awning on the near side of the street. His car was in a lot just around the corner.

"Wait!" She stopped and twisted around. "I gave Julia a ride—"

"I'm sure she's fine!" The rain picked up. Lightning streaked in closer. "I saw Lance a little while ago."

Meg shoved the hair from her face. "I can't just leave her—"

"You have to," he said, tugging her toward the parking lot. "We've got to get out of here before—"

They didn't. The sky broke open and the rain came down.

Before they could take two steps, they were soaked.

"Come on!" he called as the rain pelted them and a nearby tin roof groaned. He fumbled for his keys, shoving his hand into a pocket plastered to his body. At the car he let her in, then dashed around to his side.

The second the door closed, they both started to laugh.

"Oh my God," Meg whispered, hugging her arms around her chest. "Why does it always have to do this?"

He couldn't tell if she was annoyed, pissed or amused. "You want the simple answer?" he asked as he flipped the engine and the wipers began slapping at the rain. "Or the real one?"

She shoved at the mass of damp hair falling against her face. "You have to ask?"

No, he didn't. "It all comes down to warm, moist air," he said, squinting to see against the thick veil of rain. Slowly, he pulled onto the street—or at least what he thought was the street. "When it starts to rise into the atmosphere and slams into colder air—"

Her quick playful swat stopped him cold. He glanced to his right, found her glaring at him with "you brat" glowing in her eyes.

God he loved when she looked at him like that, all lighthearted and amused.

It had been a damn long time.

"Okay, okay," he said, making his way almost as if

by autopilot toward their house. "We'll stick with the bottom line—it's springtime and you're in Texas."

Her lips twitched. "We," she said. "*We're* in Texas."

And the raw violence of the storm still charged him up. It rained in Scotland, sometimes a lot. But it was just that, a rain. And usually a cold one. Thunderstorms came around every now and then, but they were remedial compared to the show the sky put on every March through May in Texas.

Rain and pea-size hail streaked down in horizontal slants, the wind shredding the stoic old oaks. The big trees swayed and small ones bent; new foliage was stripped from the branches and transformed into torpedoes. Lightning flashed and flickered and pulsed like some kind of crazy special effect. Thunder boomed and rattled and shook.

It took close to twenty minutes to complete a ten-minute drive.

At their house, Russell and Meg dashed hand in hand from the rental car, unsuccessfully dodging an obstacle course of debris and puddles. Russell took the three steps across the porch in one long stride, yanking open the screen door and letting a drenched Meg pass. Head down, she darted around him and out of the driving rain, again wrapping her arms around herself as she stopped just short of the front door.

Only then, when the shelter of the porch muted the worst of the storm, did he hear the laughter.

At first he thought it was just an auditory illusion, a trick of the wind whirring through the porch and slapping against the screen. Then he noticed the way Meg was hunched into herself and thought—

He didn't know what he thought. That she was hurt. That she'd tripped or twisted her ankle, that she'd been nailed by a piece of debris. He was across the porch in a heartbeat, reaching for her.

But then she twisted toward him—and her laughter stopped him cold. "Omigod, would you look at us?" she muttered, shaking her arms like a soaked animal. "We're like two drowned rats!"

He wasn't sure what drove him. The glow in her eyes, or the sudden blast of heat from somewhere long forgotten.

"I'd hardly call you a rat," he said, openly appraising the way her scoop-neck top clung to her body, the droplets of rain sliding between her breasts. "Maybe a…"

"What?" she asked, and the glow in her eyes darkened. "Something exotic and dangerous?"

Damp hair clung to her neck, drawing him closer, making him wonder what it would feel like to touch, to slide it back and linger. "Is that what you want? Exotic?"

Dangerous.

Her smile shifted from little girl to something a whole lot less innocent. "A *leopard*." She laughed as if the idea had just come to her. "Strong and beautiful and fast—"

She kept talking. He was sure she did. He could hear the enthusiasm in her voice, just as he had all those years ago in New York, when he'd told himself over and over all the reasons he should stay away from the girl who always had a question—and a smile. He was only at Columbia on a temporary assignment. His time there was short. Soon he would move on. She was younger, not very experienced, impressionable. *A student.* That's why *she* looked at him the way she did…why *he* found her smile so infectious.

He watched her now, soaked to the bone and shivering, going on and on about leopards and Africa and strength and dominance, all the while shoving impatiently at the hair plastered to her face.

That wasn't what he wanted, the impatience. He wanted to go in slow, to touch tentatively at first, to feel and taste, explicit deliberation giving way to reckless need.

"Russell?"

Through the yellow glow of the porch light they'd installed a lifetime before, the invitation in her gaze damn near destroyed him.

"You better get inside." His voice was rough, hoarse, barely audible over the rain. Clearing his throat, he tried again. "Get out of those wet clothes—" The image streaked in like the lightning around them, of her, of Meg, *his wife,* getting out of her clothes and turning to him, reaching for him.…

Beyond the sanctuary of the porch, the persistent wind whipped the rain into a frenzy. But an odd stillness settled between them as Meg lifted her eyes to his—and he flat-out forgot to breathe.

"What about you?"

Three simple words. That's all they were. A logical question. They were, after all, soaked to the bone. The rain was cold, the wind cutting, the roads nearly impassable. He needed—

"I should go," he said.

Something dark and unreadable shifted through her gaze. "No."

"Meggie—"

"You can't," she said. "The roads are flooding. It wouldn't be safe."

He didn't trust himself to move. He didn't trust himself not to. "I have to."

She just kept gazing up at him, looking as if she'd never seen him before, just as she'd done all those years before, when he'd shown up unannounced in Pecan Creek. They'd said their goodbyes in New York. Months had gone by. He'd told himself to stay away, leave her alone. But one hot summer afternoon he'd walked into her office, lounging in the doorway as she looked up with the most irresistible combination of shock and discovery shining in her eyes. He'd wanted—

So much. It all. Her. Them. Their life. *Everything.*

Walking away had not been part of the plan.

Now a few stray strands of damp hair fell against the sides of her face. "No," she whispered. "You don't."

"Meggie." Her name burned on the way out. "I should—"

"Don't." The word was soft, quiet, more breath than voice. With it she moved, lifting her hands to the sides of his face, touching gently, tentatively. As if she expected him to vanish in the heartbeat before contact.

"Stay," she whispered as she lifted her eyes to his, and everything inside him started to burn. *"Please."*

Maybe he moved first. Maybe she did. He didn't know, didn't much care anymore. Their mouths came together in a fusion of want and greed and denial, of hurt and regret, but most of all, need. There was no tenderness. No hesitation. No years between them. No broken promises, no pain. Crushing her to him, he backed her against the door and tangled his hands into her damp hair, stunned by the feel of her own hands against his face, her fingers searing as her mouth welcomed.

He pulled her close, held her tight, felt himself start to drown. This was what he remembered when he closed his eyes in bed at night, when he twisted alone in thin cotton sheets in faraway places. This is what he'd remembered, what he'd taught himself to forget. *His wife*. Opening to him. Giving.

Wanting.

CHAPTER THIRTEEN

EVERYTHING BLURRED. The storm faded, the night deepened, the dream seduced. Somewhere inside a muted voice warned Meg to pull away, break away. But she could no longer figure out why. There was only Russell and a need she'd never thought to feel again. Somehow she'd forgotten. She'd forgotten the anticipation and urgency, the blinding greed, the way a simple look, a touch, could make everything inside her melt.

But she remembered now, and she wanted. She wanted the anticipation and the urgency. She wanted the melting. She wanted his hands, his mouth…*him*.

The realization rocked her, drove her. It had been so long.…

She wasn't sure what made her pull back. To see him, she thought. To look into his eyes and know that he was real, that this was real. With her hands she found his face, with her fingers she explored. All the while he watched her, his lips parted, the dark green of his eyes burning with a near-unbearable combination of hunger—and awe.

It was the awe that got her, drove her. No one else had ever looked at her like that. No one else had ever made her want like that, made her feel as though she'd shatter into a thousand jagged pieces if he didn't touch her.

Love her.

"Russell," she whispered. Or at least she thought she did. Maybe she merely mouthed the words. She wasn't sure…didn't care. Through the haze she only knew that Russell was kissing her again, and that all those little cracks in the dam were about to give way.

Somehow they made it inside. Somehow they made it through the darkness to the room they'd shared as man and wife. The room they'd painted together, stopping somewhere deep in the night to make love. The room where they'd laughed together, slept together, loved together. The room where—

She wasn't sure exactly how she ended up in his arms with her legs locked around his waist, didn't much care. Not when she could feel the warmth of his body, the strength. She ran her hands along the wet T-shirt plastered to his back, wanted nothing more than to feel flesh instead.

They moved as one. Wanted. As one.

Mindlessly she yanked at the damp cotton, shoving it up to his shoulders. And then it was gone, discarded on the rug below, leaving only the hard planes of his body. Sliding her mouth from his, she kissed her way along the whiskers at his jaw to his neck, down to the smooth muscles of his chest. All the while she couldn't stop touching, exploring. *Wanting*.

Beneath her fingertips, the warmth of his body, the strength, fed that dark, lonely place inside her, the place she'd taught herself not to acknowledge. Now the cascade of forgotten emotions and desires blotted out everything else. All those nights alone… The hours spent walking barefoot through the empty house…sitting down by the creek, staring into the darkness with a bottle of wine—

Again she pulled back, gazing through the shadows at the harsh, painfully familiar lines of her husband's face.

"So beautiful," he whispered through the silence. *"So goddamn beautiful."*

The salty sting in her eyes caught her by surprise. She would have sworn there were no more tears.

"Hey now," he said with a gentleness that almost sent her to her knees. His hand lifted then, slow, soft, a brush of his thumb beneath her eyes. "What's this?"

She blinked hard, smiled through the tight squeeze of her heart. "Tonight…" Against the smooth curve of his chest, her hands stilled. "I—I…" The words jammed in her throat.

She wouldn't let that happen.

Knew they needed to be said.

"I wanted it to be you."

Very little light made it into the big room, only the soft glow from a night-light by the armoire, and the occasional flicker of lightning through the twin windows. But it was enough. Enough to see him stiffen, to see the confusion streak across his face.

"At the auction," she said in answer to his unspoken question. "I…" It shouldn't have been so hard. This man was her husband. She'd known him as intimately as a woman could know a man. Loved him even deeper. "I saw you at the back of the room." The jumble of anticipation came back to her, the way her imagination had started to soar.

"It was like all those years ago," she told him, each word, each revelation, easier than the one before. "At Columbia. I was that girl again, and you—"

His hands framed her face. "What?"

"You were standing there…" Much as he stood here

now, except then he'd still been wearing a shirt. "And I wanted…"

His thumb feathered along her lower lip. "What?" His voice was rough, almost painful to hear. "What did you want?"

She looked up at him, at the dark light in his eyes, the hollow of his cheeks and the swell of his bottom lip, lower to his chest. Lower—

"This," she said, answering not with words, but by returning her mouth to his. Just a soft kiss at first, a gentle hello as he stood there unmoving. *"And this…"* she murmured, opening to him as she did so, feeling the breath shudder from her as he, in turn, opened to her. *"You."*

The rough sound that broke from his throat thrilled her. "Do you have any idea," he rasped, pulling back a fraction, just enough so that their mouths hovered and their eyes met. "Any idea at all what it did to me to see you with that man?"

She hung there, absorbing the feel of his hands moving along her body, sliding low to cup her bottom— and press. She could feel him then, the full length of him, and something deep inside started to beg.

"Mine," he murmured against her open mouth. "That's all I could think."

"Yours," she echoed as his hands shifted to the front of her pants and worked at the top button. *His.*

It all seemed so easy. So natural. A rhythm as intrinsic as the flow of her breath and the thrum of her blood. Eyes wide-open, she leaned into him and put her mouth to his chest, closed around one wide flat nipple. There she suckled, using her tongue as her hands worked with the fly of his jeans. She shoved the damp fabric down his thighs, letting him take over to kick free. Through the veil of the dream she kissed and licked and touched. Discovered. *Him*. Her husband.

All of him.

"Meggie," he whispered in that way that was all his, part ragged breath, part poetry, transforming her name into an intimate and binding vow. Only then did she realize that she, too, stood naked. She stepped into him, sliding her arms around his waist as they staggered toward the big bed.

There, where they'd made love so many times, in darkness and in daylight, in joy and sorrow, hope and desperation, he yanked back the thick comforter and eased back the sheets, lowering her to the cool mattress. She urged him to follow, wanting him, all of him, as intimately as possible.

He needed no urging. He lowered his knee and hovered over her, lifting a hand to smooth her hair against the pillow. "So beautiful," he said again, and through the flood of emotion, she smiled, tugged for him to come closer.

He did, lowering himself to her, gently, first with his mouth, then with his body. They came together slowly, kisses giving way to touch, the slide of hands and mouths. She was a grown woman. She'd made love with this man hundreds of times. But when his hands found her breasts and his fingers began to flick along her nipple, she cried out in discovery, arching into him—and wanting more. He obliged, using his mouth and his tongue to drive her to the edge.

She'd forgotten. Somehow…she'd actually forgotten.

Now she remembered. All of it. *Everything*. Twisting beneath him, she lost herself in the feel of him, sliding her hands along the strength of his body until she found him, hot and hard and ready. There she cupped and claimed, driven by the thrill of discovery.

It was all so easy.

And when he slid on top of her and took her hand, when he threaded his fingers with hers and whispered her name, lifting her arms over her head and pulling back to look at her, to hold her eyes with his own as he pushed inside her, something simply shattered.

"Always," she whispered as his mouth again took hers and his hips started to move. "Yours."

Memory fused with reality, tangling, twining, twisting—until only the dream remained. They came together there, in the sanctity of the room they'd once shared, while beyond the window, the violence of the rain and the wind gradually gave way to the soft silvery glow of a new moon.

THE SPARROWS WOKE HER. They'd nested just outside the bedroom window, in one of the big crepe myrtles she'd never gotten around to pruning during the winter. She'd found the nest the week before, when their jubilant morning song had intruded upon the few of hours of sleep Charlotte had finally allowed.

Meg didn't want to open her eyes. She didn't want to get up. All she wanted was to burrow deeper into the drugging warmth and sleep a few days longer. Her body thrummed, ached. If she didn't know better, she'd think she'd spent the night—

Making love.

Abruptly the cobwebs of sleep cleared, and memory zapped into focus. Russell. Standing at the back of the pavilion, isolated somehow, despite the crowd swarming around him. Russell inserting himself between her and

Blackstone. On the Ferris wheel. The storm. Running through the rain. Standing on the porch, drenched.

The overwhelming need to touch—taste.

Inside, in his arms—in their bed. Coming together, over and over again. Feeling him on top of her, inside her.

Wanting more.

For a long moment Meg lay without moving, acutely aware that he was still there, pressed up against her. Naked. That she was naked. That if she so much as breathed the wrong way, he would wake. And if he woke up, he'd reach for her again.

He'd always had a thing for making love in the morning.

She opened her eyes, stared through the hazy glow of early morning toward the bathroom, where their clothes lay discarded against the Persian rug they'd fallen in love with several years before. When was the last time—

She didn't know. She had absolutely no idea when she'd last reached for him, *wanted* him.

But last night she'd done more than that. She'd *needed* him.

Carefully, she eased away from him, one breath at a time. She did not want him to wake up, was not ready to see him, that slow burn in his eyes, the blistering awareness of the way she'd run her mouth along his body....

The memory shocked her. Never in a million years had she thought they'd be together like that again. Never had she considered she could let go like that. Want like that. Never had she believed they could find their way back to each other.

But she'd dreamed.

Sometimes when she'd fallen into the deepest, darkest, most vulnerable depths of sleep, she'd let herself forget, and she'd dreamed. She'd dreamed that Russell was there, and the past was gone. That it hadn't happened. That he'd never left for Africa, and that Hope had never died.

Throat tight, she slipped from beneath the covers and made it to the bathroom, where she put a hand to her stomach and drew a deep breath. She'd never imagined—

That was it. Despite the dreams, she'd never imagined it could be like that again. That *they* could be like that again. During the two years that he'd been gone—

She looked in the mirror, lifted a hand to streak down her neck to her breast. She'd welcomed him, given to him as if not a day had passed.

But in the soft glow of the morning sun, it was uncertainty she saw staring back at her. Fear that whispered through her. She'd moved on with her life. She had Charlotte to consider. She couldn't let herself become vulnerable again, couldn't risk falling apart. She had responsibilities—

She blinked, spun toward the bedroom, where the digital clock on the small table read 9:04.

She had a festival meeting at nine-thirty, a status check to see what, if any, changes needed to be implemented before the gates opened at noon. After the storm the night before...

Whirling into motion, she turned on the shower and ran to grab some clothes from the closet. Fifteen minutes later she had her makeup on, her hair mostly dry, and was running from the bedroom.

She didn't let herself look back.

HE KNEW THE SECOND SHE LEFT. Half-asleep, he'd felt her slip from bed, waited for her to come back. The first one up always made the coffee. The one still in bed never stayed alone for long.

When he heard the door close, he bolted from bed and grabbed his jeans, fought his way into them as he reached the front porch. He lunged into the cool slap of early morning just as Meg backed her SUV into the street and drove away.

The quick twist to his gut made no sense. It was Saturday, just a little after nine in the morning. They'd hardly slept the night before.

Back inside, he found her briefcase gone—and a scrawled note on the counter.

Festival meeting…be back soon.

The quiet of the house pulsed around him. He stood in the stillness of the kitchen, staring at the stainless-steel appliances they'd picked out together. The once-spotless surfaces now sported little handprints and smudges. Pictures of Charlotte covered the refrigerator.

At the stereo, he found an acoustic album they'd always loved and slid it in before making his way to the refrigerator. Everything he needed was there, the eggs and the bacon, the cheese, the onions and the tomatoes.

Everything was in the same place. He found his favorite skillet, the measuring cups in the drawer by the stove, the glass mixing bowl and chopper in the cabinet under the island. And with the sun filtering through the window, he went to work on an omelet, just as he'd done dozens of times before.

For the first time in years, he felt at home.

Sweet God, he'd never imagined he'd be standing like this again, barefoot in his own kitchen. He had not wanted to come here, back to Pecan Creek. He had not wanted to see her again, the cool indifference in her eyes. To look at her and know—to remember. He'd never imagined she would reach for him. Want him.

Love him.

The memory seared through him. He could see her still, feel her still, reaching for him—opening to him. Her hands, her mouth, sliding along his body. Giving—taking. There'd been no walls, no barriers.

For the first time since before Hope died, there'd been no hiding.

Feeling the burn all over again, Russell checked the omelet before reaching for a plate. He was halfway to the old farmhouse table when he heard a car door. Surprised she was back so soon, he set the plate down and strode toward the front door.

But it was not Meg's SUV that sat in the driveway.

It was Tyler's truck.

"HE'S GONE."

Standing in the doorway to Julia's office, Meg frowned. She'd just finished up with the committee meeting and was heading home when she noticed her cousin's vintage T-bird in the *Gazette*'s parking lot. She'd started to drive right on by, but an incredible need to talk had drawn her inside instead.

After the way she'd bared herself to Russell the night before, the thought of seeing him again made her feel ridiculously shy for a woman who'd made love with this man hundreds of times.

But once inside, the sight greeting her sent all that slamming to the background.

Julia sat behind her desk, staring out the window. The last time Meg had seen her, Julia had been clad in a long trench coat and sunglasses, sneaking around the festival like an undercover operative in pursuit of her prey.

Now Julia's normally glossy hair was tangled against her unusually pale face. Dark circles rimmed her eyes. Her lips were dry. And her clothes...they were the same tailored slacks and silk blouse that she'd worn the night before.

And Meg's imagination could do nothing but race to some pretty dark places. "Who's gone? Blackstone?"

"No." Julia's voice was barely more than a rasp. "Lance."

"Lance? What are you talking about?" What did she mean...gone?

"I found him..." Julia said, her voice chillingly robotic. "At the festival..." She paused, looked from Meg back to the window. "Behind the Fun House." This time her voice, the words, broke. "With Marybeth."

Meg brought a hand to her mouth as she swallowed, searched for words. Lance...with another woman. Disbelief came first...followed by the slow bleed of anger.

"The new English teacher?" she asked.

Julia pressed her lips together, nodded. "They were going at each other like two dogs in heat."

"Oh, honey," Meg said, finally moving, hurrying across the office to kneel beside her cousin's chair and taking her into her arms, holding her tight. Julia and Lance had been together since high school, the couple most likely to couple. They'd married after their freshman year of college, had been together ever since.

There'd been an easiness between them, almost as if they were best friends.

Maybe too much like best friends.

"I'm so sorry," Meg whispered.

Julia pulled back from Meg's arms, her expression horribly blank. "He says...he says she makes him feel... alive."

Meg cringed.

"Like a man," Julia went on in that same monotone voice. "And that I...don't."

It was a lot to take in. "He's an idiot," Meg said, framing her cousin's face with her hands, "if he can't see what a wonderful woman you are."

Julia's smile was strained, forced...but in it shone a lifetime of gratitude. "I don't know what to do," she whispered. "I don't... I can't undo..."

"This isn't about undoing," Meg said, for the first time seeing it all so clearly. Julia and Lance's marriage had been in trouble for a while, but she knew her cousin had been too absorbed by the day-to-day of living to see the signs. Just as Meg had failed to see the signs.

No, no one could undo the past. No one could erase mistakes. You could only pick up the pieces and go forward. Sometimes it took time. Sometimes it took space.

But it always, always took an extraordinary leap of faith.

"It's about seeing what's left," Meg whispered. "And I'm here to tell you, it's more than you think."

MEG UNFASTENED CHARLOTTE from her car seat and propped her on her hip, holding her keys in one hand and the white bag in the other. As so often happened, the rain from the night before left a brilliant storm-washed morning in its wake, with ridiculously blue skies and a slightly cool breeze. Tree debris littered the sidewalks and Meg's petunias were flattened, but she smiled anyway.

It was a great day to have a festival.

She hadn't wanted to leave Julia. She'd stayed for just shy of an hour, talking, mostly listening, until Lori had arrived and Meg had slipped out. From her mother's house she'd retrieved Charlotte. From Uncle Ralph's she'd secured a picnic lunch. Now she only needed Russell.

Really, after all the hurt and disappointment, the broken promises and shattered dreams, it was as simple as that.

She only needed Russell.

His rental car remained parked in the street. "Let's go find Uncle Rusty," she quipped to Charlotte. Her mother had bypassed the pink pants and matching top Meg had packed, dressing the baby instead in a gorgeous floral dress with matching frilly bloomers.

"Get ready to knock some socks off," Meg said, opening the front door to the house.

She wasn't sure what she was expecting, but the music washed over her the second she walked inside. Neil Young, she recognized, smiling. He'd always been one of their favorites.

It was pushing noon, but the house still seemed sleepy. There was a stillness to the air, shadows in place of lights.

"Russell?" she called, emerging from the foyer into the family room with the wriggling baby on her hip. "Easy there," she teased, taking Charlotte's hand before she could grab a fistful of Meg's hair. "You don't want to—"

He stood in front of the big picture window overlooking the backyard, framed by a pair of brocade curtains with his back to her. Faded jeans rode low on his hips, but his chest and his feet were bare.

"There he is," she said, dropping the diaper bag onto a wing chair as she passed. And Charlotte literally lit up.

"Dada-dada," she cooed, squirming to get out of Meg's arms.

But Russell did not turn around.

Slowing, Meg eased Charlotte to the hardwood floor and held her hands, letting go when she steadied. "Dada-dada," Charlotte squealed, toddling forward like a drunken sailor. Two steps, three, four...

She fell forward, grabbing on to Russell's leg.

Meg saw him stiffen as if he'd just been struck by something much sharper, much more lethal than a twenty-pound toddler—and all the gooey bliss she'd been feeling congealed into an inexplicably cold knot.

Finally Russell moved. He scooped Charlotte up in his arms, lifting her for a soft, sweet kiss to her forehead. "Hello, poppet."

And finally Meg breathed. But the awkward undercurrent continued to throb through her. "Hey," she said, searching for the right words. The right tone. Last night they'd been as intimate as a man and woman could be.

She wasn't sure what the sunrise had brought.

"I stopped by Ralph's," she said, watching Charlotte rub her hand against the whiskers at Russell's jaw. "I had him make up some of those shrimp po-boys you like. Thought we could go out to the flower fields and—" He hadn't looked at her yet. She'd been home for five minutes, talking. And he had not turned to face her.

She didn't want to ask—but knew she had to.

"Russell?" she said, and her heart slammed so hard it echoed through her blood. "What's wrong?"

Now he turned, and now he looked straight at her.

And before he even spoke, she started to bleed.

"Tyler was here."

Three words. That's all they were. But the rigid control, the absolute iron lock on any and all emotion in his voice told her that they concealed a whole lot more. Tyler had been there. Tyler, Charlotte's father...

It was all she could do not to run and scoop Charlotte back into her arms. "Did he say what he wanted?"

"He did."

What had started as a trickle of unease quickly flashed into all-out panic. "Russell...you're scaring me."

Too late she realized that it wasn't a lack of emotion, but a tight, ugly tangle. "He came to me," Russell said, very slowly. Very, very quietly.

A quiet that Meg remembered too well.

The quiet that always preceded the storm.

The same quiet he'd given her the night he walked out the door.

"He came to me," he said again. "*This kid*. He came to me and asked me if I thought Charlotte was safe with you."

The step she took backward was pure cold instinct.

"*Safe with you*," he said again, as if she hadn't heard the first time. All the while Charlotte babbled and batted at his face.

He made no move to stop her.

Meg wasn't even sure he was aware.

"How the goddamn hell do you think that made me feel?" he snapped, and his eyes flashed with a violence she'd never seen before. Not from him. "I didn't have a fucking clue what he was talking about."

But in that one horrible moment, Meg did.

Sometimes she had nightmares. She'd be alone in the dark of her bedroom, and from the family room, she'd hear a window break. She'd hear footsteps, breathing, and she'd know she needed to run. She'd know her life depended on it.

But she could no more move than she could breathe.

Meg stood there now, and knew. She didn't need to hear the words. She saw it in the way he looked at her, a coldness so different from the warmth of the night before.

"Ainsley told him," she whispered, as much to herself as to him.

"Yes," Russell said, so vacant and distant. "She did."

Meg closed her eyes.

"She was scared," Russell said, and finally, finally more emotion leaked into his voice. "Confused," he said. "Worried that you would drink too much and do something stupid and hurt yourself."

The revelation shattered her. Ainsley had never said a word to Meg. They'd spent hours together, talking about everything under the sun. But her sister-in-law had never let on that she knew about Meg's shame.

Maybe that was why she invited Meg over so often. Maybe that was why she was always suggesting they go to dinner or catch a movie....

"My God, Meg!" Russell said, and her eyes flew open, and immediately she wished they hadn't. "You made her promise to never speak of you to me! What the hell was she supposed to do? She wasn't even twenty years old and you piled *that* onto her?"

She'd never thought about it like that. "Russell—"

"How much, Meg? How often? Alone?" he asked. "Or in bars?"

He made it sound so dirty. "You don't understand—"

But he was in no mood to listen. "When were you going to tell me?" he demanded. "When were you going to tell me, damn it?"

She stared at them, at man and child, and felt the squeeze clear down to her bones. She'd known, of course. She'd known he would eventually find out. And she'd known from the moment they made love that she had to be the one to tell him.

But like so many other times in their marriage, times when it had mattered, she'd chosen avoidance over confrontation.

"Nothing has changed, has it?" he rasped, and in his arms, Charlotte started to cry. "It's okay," he said softly, bouncing her slightly to soothe her. When he looked back at Meg, the passion was gone from his face, his voice. But the disgust remained. "You still hide from what you can't face. And you still don't trust me enough to let me help."

Temper flared. "Yes," she said tightly, refusing to tuck tail and run. "I should have told you." But he had a hell of a lot of nerve standing in judgment. "But where do you get off being so sanctimonious? As I recall you're the one who walked out the door."

He'd made it damn clear "through good times and bad" was not what he'd signed up for.

His eyes flashed. Never looking away, he lowered a

squirming Charlotte to the floor. He tried to get her to stand, but she dropped to her knees and powered over to a tower of wooden blocks.

All the while Russell kept his eyes on Meg. "Is that how you remember things?" he asked. But before she could answer, he rolled right on. "Because it's sure as hell not what I remember. I remember when we lost our baby," he said. "I remember holding you, and loving you, and trying like hell to be there for you." A shadow crossed his face. "But how could I be there for someone who was already gone?"

He might as well have slapped her.

"I was here for months afterward," he said, the light streaming in the window making his eyes look so green they glowed. "Months when you would barely look at me, much less let me touch you. And I'm here now, aren't I? That was me last night, Meg. In bed, making love to you."

It was all coming undone, the carefully woven threads of the life she'd rebuilt. She'd spent two years learning to stand tall and strong. She hated that all it took was Russell walking back into town to throw her so far off track.

"Why?" he asked as the song from the CD player changed. "*Why* is it so goddamn hard for you to meet me halfway? *Why* didn't you want me to know what happened while I was gone—what the hell did you think I was going to do?"

She angled her chin, narrowed her eyes. No way was she going to let him act as though she was the only one with a stake to lose. "Because of Charlotte. I was scared you would take her."

He winced. "Jesus Christ, Meg. What kind of monster do you think I am?"

"You left," she said, hating how her voice thickened on the words. After all these months, the echo of shock lingered deep, deep inside. This man she'd loved, this man she'd depended on, had simply walked out the door.

Coming back couldn't take away the pain that had ensued. "You left," she said again, this time a little quieter.

At the end of the day, it all came down to that.

His eyes darkened. "You didn't want me to stay."

"Time, Russell! That's all I wanted. Time and space to breathe, to heal. But you didn't want—"

"I wanted my wife!" he shouted, and, seated on the floor nearby, banging two blocks together, Charlotte started to slam them harder. Louder. "How many times do I have to tell you that? *I wanted my wife.* But you left, Meg. Maybe not this house, but you left our marriage long before I walked out that door."

Her throat burned. Her chest squeezed.

"Russell." Just saying his name hurt. So did looking at him standing there in nothing but his jeans and remembering how less than twelve hours before she'd run her mouth along his chest, kissing and savoring. She'd forgotten how good it felt to touch and be touched. Hold and be held.

Love…and be loved.

Once she would have found some way to diffuse everything, going over to Charlotte or deciding it was time to fix dinner. But the woman she'd become had learned that avoidance got you nowhere.

Sometimes you had to strike back.

"I was trying to be strong," she said, but inside she'd been shriveled up and dying. Now she crossed to him, refused to let her hands shake as she reached out. "To hold on and…"

He didn't let her finish. He didn't let her touch him, either. He lifted his hands and stepped back, the warning a hard glitter in his eyes. "You don't want to touch me right now."

She swallowed. "Don't tell me what I do and don't want," she snapped back. "You lost that right the moment you walked out the door."

"I told you I would stay," he muttered in that same awful, quiet voice. *"Goddamn it, I told you I would help make sure Tyler didn't take Charlotte away."* He paused as a hard breath ripped through him. "But even then you couldn't be bothered to tell me the truth."

"I was scared!" But she could tell the explanation was falling on deaf ears. "What do you think it was like for me, having you suddenly appear back in town? I didn't know what you wanted…what you thought—if I could trust you. I didn't know—"

"No, *I* didn't know," he said. "I didn't know what a fool I was, letting myself get blinded by the sight of you and Charlotte." He glanced at her now, still sitting near the sofa with the blocks in her hands. "I should have just taken her and gotten out of here."

Everything inside Meg went very still. "Taken her?" She took a step back, instinctively positioning herself between him and his sister's child. "Is that what you meant by settling Ainsley's affairs?"

"Meg…she's not yours."

The words were hard and empty, and like a spear straight through her, they stopped her cold. "No," she whispered. "She's all I have."

CHAPTER FOURTEEN

Eleven months ago

"Meg...ye're here."

In the doorway to the beautifully decorated room, she hesitated. Outside the sun was not yet up. The rest of the hospital was quiet, sleepy. But here the lights were bright, almost blinding, illuminating every corner of the delivery suite, but focused squarely on Ainsley. With her hair damp and slicked back, her face clean-scrubbed, and her expressive green eyes shining, she looked more like she was recovering from a strenuous run, rather than sprawled out on a sterile bed with a monitor around the massive swell of her belly and her legs bent up in some awful-looking contraption, surrounded by three women in scrubs.

The flood of emotion came so fast Meg felt her knees buckle.

Numbly, she steadied herself. Trey had taken her home, fixed coffee while she showered and dressed. Lori had met them there.

"Where else would I be?" Meg now asked, blinking against the sudden mistiness in her eyes. Her stomach churned. "I promised—"

Ainsley's smile widened. "I knew ye'd be here," she said as another contraction hit. She writhed with it, her face contorting as her hands fisted in the sheets.

It was blind instinct that sent Meg rushing over to take her hand, squeezing.

"Hold on to me," she said, and this time, even as she blinked, the tears spilled over. *"Hold on to me."*

Ainsley was just a kid, but she was about to be a mother herself. Meg had promised…

She'd promised, but if things had played out just a little differently, if Trey hadn't found her, if she'd left with that stranger only a few minutes earlier…

The shame of it all congealed into something dark and ugly. She barely recognized herself anymore.

"I'm here," she vowed as the nurse shouted that the baby was crowning.

"I was waiting…" Ainsley murmured with absolute faith…then she could say nothing more as the doctor glided in between her legs and urged her to push.

Everything inside Meg felt like broken glass, but she held Ainsley's hand with love and strength and determination, smiling through her tears.

"You're doing so well," she promised, easing the matted red hair from her sister-in-law's face, baring smooth ivory skin dotted with a sprinkle of brown freckles.

Just a kid, she thought again. Alone…

Russell.

For a moment Meg closed her eyes in silent remembrance of all that could have been, but just as quickly Dr. Brennan was coaching again, urging Ainsley to push. Meg crouched closer, her eyes locked with Ainsley's, holding on while her sister-in-law twisted in agony, lending her support, strength, her quiet vow, until finally Dr. Brennan smiled and said, "Welcome, little one."

Throat tight, Meg turned toward them, toward the baby, the beautiful little girl with the shot of bright red hair, wriggling in the doctor's arms. There was no stopping the flood of tears. There was no stopping the flood of love. The quiet, immediate vows. She didn't even try.

She didn't want to.

There beneath the glare of the white lights, Meg looked at her niece for the very first time, so new to this world, so innocent...vulnerable—and felt the quickening clear down to her bones.

"Hello, there, poppet," she whispered, not sure where the endearment came from, but knowing—*knowing*—that it was right. "We've been waiting for you."

Present Day

SHE STOOD SO INSIDIOUSLY still Russell wasn't sure she breathed. Meg was a woman of constant motion. Rarely did she remain immobile. To see her like that now, her hair soft and falling against a face unnaturally pale, the blue of her eyes dark and bottomless...

Once he would have crossed to her and taken her into his arms, promised her everything would be okay.

Hell, he would have done that just two hours before, in those last fraudulent moments before Tyler had blown the pretend world Russell had been living in to smithereens. The drinking he could have handled. Understood, even.

It was the lie, her inability to trust him, lean on him, that threw them right back to where they'd started.

Or rather, where they'd ended.

"Meg," he said, and though anger twisted through

him, he couldn't keep the sliver of gentleness from his voice. "Do you really think a judge is going to award you custody?"

Hurt flared in her eyes. "My God…" she whispered. "Who are you?"

He stood there in the house that had once been his home, watching his niece jauntily crawl to the woman she loved like a mother—the woman Russell had tried so damn hard to build a life with.

"I'm the man who loved you," he said as Meg scooped up Charlotte and held her close, tight, as if she never meant to let her go. "The man who wanted to give you the world." He'd tried, damn it. He'd tried. "But you wouldn't let me."

He heard her sharp intake of breath, but ignored it, ignored the twist of betrayal in her eyes, and made himself walk right past her, toward the foyer, grabbing his keys from the small table as he passed.

"Where are you going?"

Her voice was hard, accusing. He heard what she didn't say. Knew what she thought.

He didn't want to turn. He didn't want to see them again, Meg and Charlotte, so beautiful and perfect together. He already had enough images seared into him.

He did it anyway, glanced back one last time. "It doesn't feel very good, does it?" Regret twisted through him. "When someone doesn't play by your rules."

This time it was she who winced. *"Russell,"* she said. "It's not about rules."

"No, it's not," he said, trying like hell not to look at the way Charlotte was grinning up at Meg. "It's about calling a spade a spade, Meg. About making sure my niece is well cared for."

The ugly truth spun out between them, echoing through the silence. Meg's eyes flared and her mouth parted as if she was going to say something, but after a few breaths she shifted her attention to Charlotte instead, gazing into the child's eyes as she reached for her hand.

And Russell turned and walked out the door. He had his reply, the kind he was so used to receiving from Meg.

Absolutely nothing.

"I DON'T KNOW HOW I'm going to do this."

Sitting in the rocking chair where she held a napping Charlotte in her arms, Meg's mother looked up. "It's not forever."

"You don't know that," Meg said, placing a handful of diapers into the travel bag. Tyler was going to be there any minute. "He's her father. He could easily decide he wants to keep her."

With a pained smile Lilah glanced back down at the peaceful child sleeping in her arms. It hurt Meg a little to see them together, her mother and the grandchild she adored, and to know that by this time next year, Charlotte might not even remember who Lilah was.

Somehow Meg had made it through the final hours of the Wildflower Festival, while her mother had stayed at the house, babysitting Charlotte. Russell had not appeared at either place.

When Meg asked her mom to spend the night, she'd said yes without asking why.

And when Meg had announced her intentions to call

Tyler, again Lilah had stood by her daughter without asking why.

Now they all three waited.

"He could," her mother said after a long silence. "But that doesn't mean you're not doing the right thing."

Meg rocked back on her heels and surveyed the room, making sure she hadn't forgotten to pack anything important. Charlotte was only supposed to be gone for a few days, but Meg wanted the transition to be as seamless as possible. That was why she'd asked her mother to accompany Charlotte to Tyler's hometown. At least that was part of the reason.

"Then why does it hurt so bad?" she asked.

"Saying goodbye usually does," her mom said in that serenely wise voice of hers. "That's just the way it is. Doesn't make it any less right."

Saying goodbye. Throat tight, Meg looked away, but saw him anyway, saw Russell walking out the door.

He had not said goodbye.

"Have you called him yet?" her mom asked.

Meg didn't need to ask who. "No."

"Honey," she said as Charlotte stirred in her arms. She cradled her closer and lowered her voice. "He has a right to know."

Meg knew that. "It's just…complicated." She'd lain in bed the better part of the night, trying to figure out how she could have been so foolish as to let him back into her heart. Nothing had changed, she reminded herself. What Russell couldn't handle Russell walked away from. It was so clear to see now. But for a few fragile hours there, she'd wanted so badly to believe.

She *had* believed.

Now, no matter how hard she tried, she couldn't scrape the memory of him from her mind, how quickly the melting green of his eyes had first gone hard, then cold.

"I'll call him later on," she said, standing to retrieve a couple of board books from the shelf.

"Honey…" Before her mom even finished the question, Meg braced herself for what she knew was coming. *"What happened?"*

Meg swallowed…hard. "I forgot how it used to be," she said, as much to herself as to her mother. The pain and the heartache, the disappointment. "Then Friday night…at the festival…" All the hurt and disappointment had just slipped away, leaving only Meg and Russell, and the way it had always been between them. *Before.*

Before they started trying for a baby.

Before years passed, and disappointment mounted.

Before making love became something clinical, to be documented and tracked.

Before the miracle of their baby, and Meg's irrational fear of letting Russell touch her, lest something happen to their baby.

Before the sonogram that changed everything…

Before Meg broke…and Russell left.

"Meg." Her mother's extraordinarily gentle eyes met hers. "I don't think you forgot," she said. "I think you remembered."

"No." That was Meg's first instinct, to deny. Pretend. But the truth bared the lie. She *had* remembered. She'd remembered what it had felt like in the beginning, and then, in the end, the mind-numbing intimacy and the excruciating vulnerability. When Russell had looked at her, touched her...

All she'd wanted was to go back. Go back to a time when the hurt wasn't there, and promises really did last forever.

"But none of that even matters now," she whispered, unable to tear her gaze from the window.

Because Tyler had just pulled into the driveway.

NIGHT FELL SLOWLY. Off to the northwest the sky flashed, but the wind promised to steer the storm clear of Pecan Creek.

"Tomorrow," Russell said, shifting his BlackBerry as he turned from the window. His suitcase sat in the corner—it wouldn't take more than fifteen minutes to pack. "Flying out of Dallas-Fort Worth early afternoon. Barring bad weather, I should be in Manhattan in time for a late dinner."

With the sunrise he'd board another plane, this one for Afghanistan.

"Call me when you land, then," the new BBC Middle East bureau chief said. Over the years, Sean had earned both Russell's trust and his friendship. "I'll brief you on the landscape."

"Will do." Russell wound down the call and crossed to his suitcase, tossed it on the gorgeous old quilt covering the bed.

Frowning, he realized he should have trusted his instinct to request a different room. Even when you went right back to the very same spot, it was no longer the same. Time changed everything.

At the closet, he yanked open the door and ripped a handful of shirts from their hangers. Crossing back to the bed, he started to fold them, but ended up cramming them into the suitcase instead.

She's all I have.

The words, the sober truth behind them, scraped. He'd stood there in the shadows of the family room, watching her with Charlotte, and something inside him had just…derailed. She'd looked so beautiful—*they'd* looked so beautiful. Charlotte may not have been Meg's biological child, but the bond between them was plain to see. The thought of that breaking, of Meg losing yet another baby, twisted him up inside.

She'd turned to alcohol. He still couldn't believe it. Nor could he believe how fully the truth had been kept from him, not just by Meg, but her mother and her friends, his own sister. If someone had just freaking told him—

He stopped, because he didn't know. He didn't know why no one had told him, and he didn't know what the hell he would have done.

But it would have been something. He would have done something, if he'd known. He would have found a way to help.

But Meg had not wanted him to know, had not wanted to let him in. Had not wanted to reach out.

Just like so many other times before.

Returning to the closet, he retrieved his running shoes and shoved them into the suitcase. He'd tried to assure Tyler that Charlotte was not in any danger from Meg, because despite everything, he couldn't really imagine that she was. He'd been here a week, and he hadn't seen the first sign of Meg being in trouble. But he had seen the unease in the boy's eyes. If the kid got a lawyer—

Russell frowned. He never should have volunteered to settle Ainsley's affairs. He should have just kept his distance. He'd been so sure that he could walk these streets again and breathe this air without all those sharp, broken pieces slicing to the bone.

He'd been wrong.

Now all he wanted to do was get on that plane tomorrow and fly back to the life he'd been building for the past two years, the one where he didn't slam into closed doors every time he turned around.

He couldn't fix Meg. He got that now. It was impossible to fix someone who didn't want to be fixed.

There would be a custody battle. And it would be ugly. He'd already called his lawyer. And in the end…

He hated the thought of what the end would bring.

More packed than not, he crossed to the antique writing desk where he'd set up his laptop. He had e-mail to check and a volatile political situation to brush up on.

He was on his fifth message when a knock from the door interrupted him. He crossed the room and pulled it open, found Liz dressed in some flowing turquoise sundress. "All packed?" she asked.

"Close enough."

"I'm going to miss having you around," she said with that sweet smile he remembered from when she'd been just a teenager. It was hard to imagine she was old enough now to run her grandparents' bed-and-breakfast. "Did Meg catch up with you?"

He stilled. "Meg?"

Liz fiddled with the clip holding back her hair. "She came by earlier, said she'd catch up with you later."

"No," he said, then remembered the call that had come in when he'd been confirming his travel plans. He hadn't switched over and had forgotten to check his messages.

"Oh, well," Liz said. "Maybe you can catch her before she goes to bed."

"Maybe," he said, but didn't exactly see that happening. He returned to his laptop after Liz left, but found himself picking up his phone instead, where one message waited.

"Russell," came her voice, notably hesitant, a little… off. "I…I came by the Manor earlier but you weren't there. I…I thought you should hear this from me."

The cold trickle of unease was immediate.

"I…I let Tyler take Charlotte."

She might as well have punched him in the gut.

"I realized you were right. And I don't want a fight. That won't do any of us any good. So I called him and suggested he spend some time with her."

Holy God.

"He picked her up today," Meg said in a voice he hardly recognized, all stoic and stripped bare, as if she had to manually produce each word. "My mother went with them just…just in case."

The blast of cold came hard, and it came fast. He could see her, see Meg holding Charlotte…feeling as if she had to hand her over.

Because he'd vowed she would never be deemed fit to keep her.

"I…I think it's the right thing," she said, but Russell was already across the room, shoving his feet into his shoes.

He didn't need to hear any more. And without really knowing why, he ran.

THE OFFICES OF THE *Gazette* were empty. He didn't really expect to find her there, but the paper was on the way, so he checked. He'd found her there before, after all. After losing Hope, she'd often worked deep into the night, losing herself in the demands of the paper.

Once he'd found her just before sunrise, asleep at her desk.

Darkness blanketed the town, but the traffic lights didn't seem to care that barely anyone was on the street. They continued to turn red as soon as he approached. The first two he obeyed.

The last three he did not.

Meg had called Tyler. She'd let him take Charlotte… Charlotte whom she loved with every breath of her body.

Meg had let her go.

He rounded the corner to their street, saw her car in the driveway. But the punishing echo inside him did not quiet. Gunning the engine, he closed the distance to their house and pulled alongside the curb, turned off the car. Threw open the door.

Strode toward the house.

It was dark. That was his first thought. Quiet. Completely normal for this hour of night. Maybe she was already asleep. Or maybe she was just in the shower or bathtub, unwinding from a long day. She wasn't answering her phone because she didn't want to talk to anyone.

But when he reached for the screen door he found himself yanking, and when he lifted a hand to knock, he slammed his fist to the hardwood instead.

Nothing. No sound. No movement. The door remained shut, Meg inside. Him…outside.

It was so damn familiar.

He knocked again…louder.

Called her name.

Still nothing.

On impulse he pulled out his BlackBerry and punched her number as he crossed to the front window. At first he'd thought the house dark, but now he saw the soft glow from the kitchen—and the big antique farmhouse table Meg had just had to have.

She sat with her back to him, her head on the table.

Broken glass lay all over the hardwood floor.

Russell didn't think. Didn't hesitate. He ran back to the door and shoved his hand into his pocket, pulled out his keys. It was a long shot—

The key slid right in. All this time, all this distance, and Meg had not changed the locks. He could have come home anytime, any night, and let himself in.

He wasn't sure why the discovery unsettled him.

He wasted no time on gentleness or finesse. He pushed inside and kicked the door behind him, crossed through the formal living room to the kitchen, the table. "Meg!"

She didn't stir, just continued to sit eerily still, with her head resting on the table, much as he'd found her that long-ago sunrise when she'd fallen asleep at her desk.

"Meg?" Slivers of glass crunched beneath his feet. A dark liquid stained the baby blanket peeking out from beneath a chair. A pungent smell—

He reached her, didn't understand why his hand wanted to shake. "Honey?" Going down on one knee, he put a hand to her shoulder—and saw her eyes. Beneath a scraggle of tangled blond hair, they were huge and dark…empty. Staring.

"She's gone," she whispered, and despite the absolute lack of emotion in her face or her voice, the punch of relief almost had him crushing her in his arms. Instead he trod slowly.

"I know," he said. "I got your message."

"I...I went by the Manor..."

"I know," he said again. "I'm sorry I wasn't there."

Beneath his hand, Meg's back rose and fell with deep, measured breaths. "I couldn't keep her," she said, and then she looked at him. She twisted toward him and let him see her, all of her, the dilation of her pupils and the dryness of her mouth, the lack of color in her cheeks.

Shock, he realized in a heartbeat. And again, the urge to gather her against him was punishing.

"You're right. No judge in his right mind would let me keep her."

Russell went down on both knees, using his free hand to reach for hers. She didn't fight him, didn't try to pull away, just let him curl the warmth of his fingers around the coldness of hers.

"Not true," he said, deliberately letting the cadence of his childhood slip in. Soothing, she'd always called it. Magic. "That was just anger talking, Meggie. Frustration. The truth is ye're a wonderful mother. Any judge could see—"

"I'm an alcoholic."

Three words. Three little words. That's all they were. And it wasn't as if he didn't know. But coming from her mouth, the admission rocked him, brought so much into focus...the fascinating mix of fragility and strength he'd noticed the second he came back, of reserve and determination. The way her friends worried over her— and despised him.

Because he'd walked away. Meg had been hurt,

falling, but instead of helping pick up the pieces, he'd let pride and ego get the better of him, and he'd walked out the door.

"Meg." His voice thickened around her name, and then he quit speaking, quit thinking, just let instinct take over. Let instinct guide him. He tightened his hand against hers and urged her toward him, reached for her as she slid from the chair into his arms, closed his eyes as she sank against him.

Held on…as she finally let go.

HIS ARMS WERE STRONG, his chest warm, solid. There in the shadows of the kitchen—*of the life they'd once shared*—Meg relaxed against the man she'd vowed to love forever, but had all but told to go to hell.

He dragged her closer, held her in his lap, gently started to rock her. And as she eased into him, as the steady thrum of his heart reverberated through her, the long-craved catharsis seduced her.

"I wanted our baby so badly," she said against his chest. "When we lost her…" It was hard to put into words. "There was this huge hole in my heart that I didn't know how to fill.

"After you left, it was so quiet," she whispered. "At first…" There'd been relief. So much relief. With him gone, she wasn't reminded. With him gone, she didn't have to remember. "It was liberating. I didn't have to worry about being there for you…being the wife that I didn't know how to be anymore."

He said nothing, but she felt her words ram through him, felt them in the way his throat worked against the side of her face, the way his body braced, as if in anticipation of another blow.

"But then…" She wasn't sure when or how it

happened. There wasn't one defining moment when the weight of silence had suddenly become unbearable. "The nights were the worst. The quiet."

Against the back of her head, his big hand began to stroke once again, his splayed fingers easing through tangled hair.

"I grew to hate the quiet," she said, and she couldn't stop herself, couldn't stop from tilting her face to look up, to see…him.

"There must have been a lot of that in Africa," she whispered.

His smile was like granite, but he said nothing. Didn't need to.

"It started out as just a glass of wine," she said. "Even before you left. Every couple of nights, when I got home from work. The *Gazette* had a loan called, and we had to lay off almost a third of the staff."

Stonily, he looked beyond her, toward the glow of darkness from the big window overlooking the back-yard.

"One glass became two," she kept on, careful to keep her tone neutral, as unemotional as possible. "Two turned into three."

Russell closed his eyes.

"Every few nights became every night." And Lori and Julia started to look at her a little closer, invite her over for dinner, linger…hover. Her mother had started to stop by unannounced. Even Ainsley had begun to hover. "Just to take away the edge, I told myself. Just to…help me relax."

His hold on her tightened, and when he opened his eyes, the green was bright—liquid. "I didn't know."

"I didn't want you to."

"Ainsley should have told me."

The ferocity in his voice washed through her, and for a brief moment in time, she let herself fantasize about how differently things could have turned out. If Russell had come home...would Ainsley still have gotten pregnant? Would she have died?

Would Charlotte still be the center of Meg's world?

"I thought I hid it from her," Meg said. "I didn't want..." Her sister-in-law to think poorly of her. "She needed me to be the strong one."

"You were."

Meg sucked in a sharp breath, let it out slowly. "I always thought I was protecting her." But now she knew the truth. Ainsley had known all along. She'd been the strong one, honoring Meg's secret out of love and respect, working instead through the silence of the background, using her love like an invisible lifeline.

On a deep breath, Meg again twisted to face Russell. "I almost slept with a total stranger." She wasn't sure where the words came from or why they came out... but could do nothing but try to breathe as the lines of his face tightened and the green of his eyes darkened.

His arms remained around her, his body against hers, but the tenderness congealed into something dangerously close to pain.

"The night Charlotte was born," she said, keeping her eyes on his, even though doing so, seeing him...what her words were doing to him...pierced her. "I didn't know Ainsley was in labor. I'd just had to lay off Marlene and I...I went to a bar and lost track of how much I'd had. I just wanted..."

Against her back, his hand flexed.

"You," she whispered, realizing the simple truth way too late. In all of her attempts to be brave and strong,

she'd never let herself reach for what she needed most of all. "When I didn't feel anything, I wanted to feel something...and when I felt something...I didn't want to feel anything."

She wasn't sure what she expected, for him to jerk back, condemn her, push her away. Walk away.

Instead he pulled her deeper into his arms, and cradled her. *"Meggie."*

The warm cadence of his voice drifted through her, and despite the devastation of the past thirty-six hours, the tightness inside her began to relax. "I don't know what would have happened if Trey hadn't found me."

Russell's hand was moving again, again toying with her hair. "None of that matters now."

Yes, it does, she wanted to scream, but before the words formed, the truth of his sent hers scurrying.

"The past is over," he said in that hypnotic way of his, and then he was rocking her again, slightly, slowly, in a silent, long-forgotten rhythm.

"That was it," she murmured into his chest. "That was my rock bottom. When I saw Charlotte..." She closed her eyes, living it all over again, the sheer beauty of the first time she saw her niece, the bright red hair and shocking green eyes, the sense of recognition.

"Oh, God," she cried against a fresh wave of pain. Because now she could see Tyler, too...in the shape of Charlotte's eyes, the bow of her mouth. Ainsley's soldier had looked so nervous when he'd first taken his daughter into his arms, awkward. But then Charlotte had smiled and started to babble, and Tyler had been lost.

"I can't...breathe," she whispered, hugging her arms around her waist. "I can't..."

"Yes, you can," Russell said, holding her even closer. "Yes. You. Can."

She was so tired of fighting, of trying to protect and be strong. So tired of building walls. Of holding everything inside. For once, she just wanted to let go. To exhale.

For once, she just wanted to reach out…and let Russell reach back.

"What am I going to do?" she murmured against his chest. "How am I going to live without my little girl?"

SHE'D ALWAYS LOVED SUMMER. A Texas girl, she craved warmth, had never been so cold as the summer Russell had taken her to the Highlands before their wedding to meet his family. She'd withdrawn into herself, holding herself so tight her whole body had ached. Even beneath a stack of wool blankets, she'd shivered.

Until Russell had slipped into her room, and her bed. There, with a cool damp wind assaulting his childhood home, he'd drawn her against the warmth of his naked body, and held her. Just held her. She'd turned to him, had wanted so badly to make love, but he'd just smiled that Russell-gorgeous smile of his and held her closer, kissed her gently, softly, and told her the walls were paper-thin. All through the night he'd held her, their naked bodies wrapped together beneath the blankets, and there'd been no more cold. Not until he'd slipped from bed just before sunrise.

Then the cold had come rushing back.

Floating somewhere between memory and reality, Meg twisted in the soft cotton of her sheets, drawing the covers closer. But no matter how deeply she burrowed into the thick down, she couldn't find the warmth of before. And her whole body started to shiver.

To the soft glow of the morning sun, she came awake, yanked, it felt, from somewhere warm and safe, thrust instead into somewhere bright and...cold.

She sat, clutching the covers to her chest, trying to breathe through the tightness. She blinked, squinted, tried to find focus.

And like a great big awful tidal wave, it all came rushing back. The afternoon before, Tyler and her mother, the sight of Charlotte in her car seat through the window, of the truck pulling out of her driveway.

Of the quiet, the stillness, the shaky phone call to Russell, the sound of his voice asking her to leave a message.

Of the wine, the smell and the taste, the way her hands had trembled, how she'd shoved it all from the table, sat there staring while it shattered and spilled, how she'd finally put her head to the table and let the silence take over.

Of Russell.

The pounding on the door, the rough edge to his voice, of him dropping to his knees beside her, taking her hand in his...

The warmth.

She closed her eyes, hugged her arms around her body. Not a dream, she realized. The warmth had not been a dream. The security—the comfort. The sense of...rightness. Of safety.

Of forever.

Russell had come back. Her inability to reach for him had pushed him away, but he'd come back. And he'd taken her in his arms, held her as she'd finally let go. He'd listened without judging. He'd comforted without demanding. And then he'd taken her in his arms and carried her to the bedroom—their bedroom. Headed for her dresser—

Meg opened her eyes and looked down, found a giant University of Texas jersey draping over her shoulders.

Without a word, he'd taken her hand and led her to her bed. Without a demand, he'd slid in behind her and just...held her.

All night long.

It had been the most natural communion in the world.

With the memory came a new stream of warmth. Holding on to it, Meg ignored the whisper of vulnerability and slipped from bed. The hardwood floor they'd refinished years before was cool beneath her feet as she padded from the bedroom toward the aroma of coffee drifting from the kitchen.

Three steps into the hall she stopped, turned back toward the room at the far end, with the bright spill of sunshine through the open door....

Charlotte.

The ache, the loss, took her breath away all over again.

Numbly she made her way through the family room to the kitchen, listening. For something.

But finding only quiet.

"Russell?" Her throat was dry, cottony, her voice thick from sleep.

The broken glass was gone.

She stopped beside the kitchen table, seeing only faint splotches where the wine had pooled against the floor. Every other sign, every other reminder from the night before, was cleaned away.

"Russell?" she said again, this time turning toward

the kitchen. Everything was spotless, the counters wiped down, the dishes gone from the sink: only a lone mug sat on the counter next to the full pot of coffee, and a single manila envelope.

Meg didn't know how long she stood there, barefoot in the hazy light of early morning, staring at the envelope on the counter. She only knew that she didn't want to step closer, didn't want to pick up that envelope and look inside.

Didn't want to know.

Because deep inside, in that place only Russell could touch, only Russell could heal, only Russell could destroy, she already knew.

CHAPTER FIFTEEN

"HE LEFT ABOUT AN HOUR AGO," Liz said, looking up from a sleek white laptop. Her smile was warm, sad. "Hated to see him go," she said. "I really enjoyed having him around—plus, he was a darn good guinea pig."

Meg kept herself very still, didn't want her friend to see the crush of disappointment. "Place looks great," she said. Clearly Liz had done tons of work. "When's the official grand opening?"

"Next month," she said. "If everyone—" with a quick, almost nervous, glance toward the renovated parlor, Liz brushed long, side-swept bangs from her eyes "—cooperates."

On any other day, the odd tone to Liz's voice would have made Meg smile. The Magnolia Manor, she knew, was not renowned for cooperation. Anything but. Even the fire that destroyed the original property hadn't exactly followed convention. To this day, no one knew if the inferno had been an accident or arson.

"I'm sure everything will go great," Meg said absently.

"I think so," Liz said. "At least I hope so." A little enthusiasm leaked back into her voice. "Russ said everything was perfect—even my botched attempt at French toast!"

Meg winced at the familiar form of Russell's name.

"I just can't believe he's going back to that place," Liz was saying. "You must be scared to death."

Meg's smile tightened. Russell had said goodbye to Liz. He'd told her where he was going.

"He was just here to settle Ainsley's affairs," she said, as much to herself as to Liz.

Her friend's eyes met hers, and in them Meg saw the same wisdom-of-the-ages compassion she'd seen years before, when she'd first been pregnant and Liz had volunteered to do a tarot card reading.

"Still," Liz said. "Goodbyes are never easy."

"No," Meg said quietly. "They aren't."

SHE DROVE. WITH NO REAL destination in mind, Meg veered away from the weekday congestion of the downtown Historic District, toward the quiet of the outlying country roads. She'd always found peace among the shady highways, comfort on the secluded hiking trails.

"Everything's fine," her mother said shortly before ten. "Charlotte stayed with me in the hotel last night, but we're on our way back to Tyler's parents' house right now."

"Is she…" Meg fumbled for words. "Did she sleep okay? Did she cry?"

"Megan." Lilah's voice came through the cell phone like a caress. "Don't do this to yourself, honey. Don't torture your—"

"I miss her."

"I know you do."

"And I'm so scared." Everything she'd ever wanted had been right there, waiting. All she'd had to do was reach out and hold on tight.

"Of course you're scared," Lilah said. "How could

you not be? But you just have to believe this is going to work out somehow. Tyler's folks are good people. They only want what's best for Char-Char."

The backs of Meg's eyes stung, fracturing the narrow highway in front of her into liquid prisms. "I know." Swallowing, she eased off the gas pedal, slowing as she neared a secluded dirt road to the right. "Call me if anything changes."

"You know I will."

"And give my girl a kiss from—" *Mommy* "—me."

"Always."

Tossing the phone onto the passenger seat, Meg turned from the state highway onto the quiet, unmarked road. It had been a long time. Once she'd driven this road daily. Once, Russell had driven it with her. They'd sat in silence, him behind the wheel, her in the passenger seat with her cold hands clasped in her lap. Behind them, the partially open trunk had bobbed, a young willow sapling half in, half out.

Meg's throat tightened at the memory. Turn around, she told herself, but something stronger drew her farther down the bumpy road, to the small, gravel parking lot at the end. There, a state highway department sign declared the area a historical site.

Woodenly she stopped the car and silenced the engine, pushed open the door and stepped into the warm April morning. Sunshine filtered through the trees, seemingly dancing at her feet.

The smile was automatic—and as always, it hurt.

Beyond the parking area, she made her way through the quiet hills of the state park, overgrown now with tall, wispy grasses and eager weeds, through a grove of pecan trees old and young, toward the babble of the creek just beyond.

A few miles away, this same creek ran through the town—and behind Meg's house. Normally it was barely more than a trickle. But on occasion, following heavy or prolonged rain, the water rose. Once, the current had been swift enough to carry away an abandoned car.

Now an army of wild pink buttercups swayed with the breeze, sloping down toward the creek bed…and the willow Meg and Russell had planted in honor of the baby they'd lost. Barely five feet tall at the time, the memorial now towered over twenty. The creek provided the right amount of water for the sapling to flourish, and there was just enough sunshine for it to thrive. Against the bright light Meg squinted, but the shadow remained beneath the fall of the graceful tree, tall and strong. Unmoving.

She stopped. Less than twenty feet separated them, but she could not make herself take another step, not when Russell stood beside the tree, his body painfully still as he stared out over the creek. Higher than usual, the water eddied around boulders and bramble, creating its own gurgling soundtrack.

Slowly, he turned, and his eyes met hers. And held. There was a stark isolation there, a pain she'd not seen in a long time. And in response, she did the only thing she could. She started toward him.

"You know that's illegal, don't you?" she said, glancing toward the clump of bluebonnets clenched in his hand. Dirt dangled from the roots.

"Only if I get caught," he said, and though the words were light, classic Russell, no smile formed in accompaniment.

Meg's throat tightened. She swallowed, looking up as she reached him. Sometimes she forgot how tall he was. How solid. Sometimes she forgot the way the light in his eyes could penetrate—and the wall of his chest could seduce. Even in a wrinkled black button-down and old, faded jeans, with scuffed boots on his feet, the sight of him fed that dark, lonely place inside her.

And it always had.

All she had to do was lift a hand, and she would touch him. It was what she wanted. To touch, to hold on.

This time for keeps.

But instead, she offered words.

"Two years ago when you told me you were leaving—" her mouth was dry, the words thick "—I knew I should say something...but I didn't know how." She hesitated, the breeze blowing her loose, uncombed hair against her face. Even now, all this time later, the memory hurt.

"I wanted—" *so much* "—for things to be different," she said as he continued to just stand there, more statue than man, watching her. "For us to be different. For you to hold me..."

Something sharp and volatile flashed through his eyes.

"I was paralyzed," she went on. "Numb. It's like I was locked inside my body, and no matter what I tried, what I wanted, I couldn't break through. So I watched you walk away, drive away...and I knew you weren't coming back."

The line of his jaw tightened.

"And I hated you," she said, feeling it all over again, the blanket of numbness giving way to the sting of reality. "I hated you for leaving me."

His mouth twisted. "You hated me for being there."

She didn't want his words to be true, but knew that

they were. "I was broken," she said, struggling to explain. *To understand.* "When Hope died, something inside me died, too." Hopes and dreams...innocence. "She was part of me. And I felt her, Russell. Every second of every day I knew she was there, even before I felt her move. Then she did and I—"

"She was part of me, too."

She absorbed his words like a blow. *"I know."* Every time he'd looked at her, she'd seen the pain in his eyes—and a flash of the little girl they'd lost. Every time he'd touched her, she'd felt Hope....

"I know," she said again, this time softer. *"She was us.*

"And you were right," she said now. "It was so easy to cast you as the bad guy...so much easier than looking in the mirror. You may have been the one to actually walk out the door, but...I checked out first."

In grief they'd both retreated to their own safe place, running in opposite directions, instead of to each other.

Around them the wind continued to whisper softly, toying with the thick canopy of the willow tree. Sun dappled around the wildflowers at their feet.

She'd always loved this place. *They had.*

"I've prided myself on moving forward," she said over the clamor of the birds and the water. "But from the moment you came back, I've barely been able to breathe. I immediately fell back to the way things were before, resenting you for things over and done with." Because that was...familiar. Safe. "To the point that I couldn't see what was right before my eyes." What she saw now...what she'd seen the night before, when he'd pulled her into his lap and held her.

"That *you're here*," she said, and with the words she

stepped closer. Her whole body hummed with the need to touch him. "You're here and no matter how hard I push, no matter how many dragons I throw in your path, you're just…here. Not judging, not demanding, just strong and steady." Full of that same quiet strength she'd fallen in love with a lifetime before. "Just…*here*."

Even after she'd rejected his offer to help her fight for Charlotte, even after she'd pushed him away by failing to reach out, he'd still come back the second he'd learned she'd surrendered Charlotte to Tyler.

Russell had come back.

A rough sound broke from somewhere low in his throat. "Like I wasn't before," he said with a gruffness that sent the ache in her heart knifing deeper.

"I don't want to break again," she whispered. She'd come too far. "And I'm so scared to let myself love you—" she saw him wince, saw him brace "—but I'm even more afraid of letting you go—"

He didn't let her finish. "I told myself nothing had changed. That's why I got in the car this morning. That's why I drove away. But with each mile that passed, all I could see was the way you looked at me last night."

Once, his words would have made her look away, part in shame, part in fear. But in that moment, Meg could no more have looked away than she could have walked away.

"The vulnerability," he said. "And the trust. That despite everything, you trusted me enough to let me see inside. And I couldn't do it…"

Finally he moved, finally he closed the last of the distance between them, reaching for her, pulling her into his arms and against the wall of his chest.

The sense of homecoming stole her breath. She

stepped into him and wrapped her arms around him, absorbed the feel of him.

"I couldn't walk away again," he admitted, "not when you were right. *I* was the freaking coward…walking away from the woman I loved because I didn't know how to reach her, running when I should have moved mountains to hold on." Abruptly his hands found her face, his fingers splaying out—and cradling her. Instinctively she tilted back to see him—and instinctively her heart did a long, slow free fall through her chest.

"Quitting," he said, "when I should have given you every breath I had."

She wasn't sure how she stayed standing. "Russell—"

"I could feel you slipping away," he said, and the pain in his eyes brought her even closer. She couldn't just stand there when the need to touch, to heal, swelled with every beat of her heart.

"And it killed me," he said. "I tried to reach for you, to pull you back…but everything I did just pushed you farther away, to the point where you were barely even there. I—I…"

He was a strong man, driven, full of purpose. She'd never seen him like this before, hesitant…vulnerable.

"…didn't know what you wanted from me," he said hoarsely.

And her heart slammed hard. "For you to stand by me," she said, lifting her hands to his chest and feeling the strong rhythm beneath her palm. "Like you did when Tyler first showed up. For you to hold me—" she closed her eyes a moment, let the memory wash over her "—like you did last night."

He slid a thumb to her mouth, the flash of his eyes telling her that he wanted—*needed*—to keep talking.

"I never planned to stay," he said, and against her body, she could feel the tension move through his. "When I came back…" He hesitated, let out a rough breath. "From the moment I saw you…saw Charlotte… it was like some vicious trick of fate, taunting me with the life I could have had—*we could have had*—if I'd just…stayed."

The need to comfort him drove her. The need to… fix. "Not if you'd stayed," she said, going up on her toes and brushing her mouth against his. "We needed that time…." She could see it now, could see the truth. They'd needed time, and space. To heal. To grow.

"If you'd stayed, we would have ended up destroying each other. We can have that life now, because we found each other," she whispered with a fresh salty sting in her eyes. "Because you *came back*."

The green of his eyes took on a forgotten gleam, as raw as it was powerful. "Christ, Meggie, sometimes I'd lie awake in Africa, wanting you so damn bad my whole body hurt."

She smiled through her tears. "I wanted you, too."

He winced. "I never thought I'd hear you say that again."

"I wanted you, too," she said again, this time louder. Firmer. "I still do." With the words, she slid her hands along his chest, savoring the solid strength of him. "Don't go." Buoyed by newfound courage, she lifted her eyes to his. "I couldn't say that before." But now the words felt strong—right. "Stay with me." Those words felt right, too. *"Love me."*

He muttered something—low, lilting, in the dialect of his childhood. She made out *always* and *love*—and *forever*.

And then his arms were closing around her, crushing

her to him as his mouth came down against hers, and there beside the gentle flow of the creek, beneath the graceful fall of the willow branches, all those broken, jagged pieces, the ones that had sliced and destroyed for too long, slipped back into place—and fused.

EPILOGUE

EVEN IN SLEEP, HE KNEW she was gone.

Russell Montgomery opened his eyes to the pre-dawn darkness of late summer and found the sheets tangled around his hips, the space next to him empty, the feather pillow cool to his touch. Once, when he'd existed from one hotel room to another, the realization that he slept alone would have punished him. Now a slow, easy warmth moved through him.

Waking up alone went with the territory.

He rolled from bed and headed for the hall, didn't bother with pulling on a shirt or a robe. A pair of slippers sat beside the nightstand, but he could count on one hand the number of times he'd actually worn them. Just didn't see the point.

From down the hall, the soft strains of a Gaelic lullaby drifted through the sleepy old house. He moved quietly, not wanting to disturb. Not wanting to interrupt. He'd seen a lot of beauty in his life. He'd experienced moments of awe. He was no stranger to mystery. But nothing had prepared him for the combination... those pure, naked, unguarded moments when the world seemed to stand still.

He found her at the end of the hall, in the small room with the buttery-yellow walls and soft plush carpet, with the lights off and a spill of shadows, the soft strains of lullabies the Montgomery children had listened to for generations. She sat in the rocking chair with her eyes closed, tangled blond hair falling against her face, the cotton nightshirt wrinkled—and sliding up her legs.

In her arms, Charlotte slept.

It was a simple scene, impossibly common, played out in houses all across town. A baby woke during the night. A mother came to settle her. A father watched.

But for Russell, the scene was not common at all.

Father. The word still had the power to turn him to mush.

He stood there a long moment, just watching, drinking it all in, searing the image into his memory, where so many others waited. Meg as she'd been nearly a decade before, when he'd first seen her sitting in the big lecture hall. Meg as she'd been the day he first came to Pecan Creek, when they'd made love for the first time. Meg on the day they married. Meg holding a home pregnancy test in her hands, glowing.

Meg sitting by the creek behind their house, crying.

But on top of those memories drifted new images— bright, strong images that reduced the past to shadows: Meg sitting cross-legged among the bluebonnets on the day he'd come back, rocking a sleeping baby in her arms. Meg kneeling by his sister's bed, surrounded by letters and postcards, with the oddest expression of discovery on her face. Meg standing beside the sofa they'd picked out together a lifetime before, going up on her toes to reach out to him, first with her hands, then her mouth.

The relief in her eyes when he'd joined her on the porch, when Tyler had first come to meet Charlotte.

The warmth of her hand.

Meg at the Wildflower Festival, standing at the

podium with the auction form in her hands, watching him.

Meg on the Ferris wheel with the storm pushing in behind her.

A rain-soaked Meg looking at him with the most amazing combination of trust and vulnerability and desire.

The raw courage when she'd told him what happened after he'd left…and the quiet trust when she'd let him hold her.

The naked vulnerability when he'd turned to find her standing by the old creek, with the wind whispering through her hair—and love glowing in her eyes.

But most of all, he could see her the morning two days later, when she'd opened the front door to find Tyler standing there, with Charlotte. She'd tried so hard to hold it all together, but the second Tyler had relinquished Charlotte into her arms, Meg had drawn the baby to her heart, and quietly fallen apart. Russell had joined her, sliding an arm around her waist and anchoring her against him, while Tyler explained that despite how much he loved his daughter, he could not give her what she needed most. A family. A home. A mother.

Meg.

Tyler had visited a handful of times since then, content with his new role as special uncle. Russell's parents had visited, as well. And they, too, had realized where Charlotte belonged.

Now in the predawn quiet, Russell watched them, Meg and Charlotte, mother and child. And standing there, he knew there was nothing he wouldn't do, no mile he wouldn't walk, no test he wouldn't confront, to keep them safe, keep them his.

Keep his family together.

This time for keeps.

"Hey."

The soft, sleepy voice startled him. Through the shadows he realized that somewhere along the line Meg had opened her eyes. "Hey, yourself."

"Everything okay?" she asked, brushing a soft kiss to the top of Charlotte's head.

Such a simple gesture, but like so many others, he knew the image, the rightness of it, would stay with him.

"You're beautiful…you know that?" he said, starting toward them. "Both of you."

"I'm happy," she whispered.

At the rocking chair he stopped and went down on one knee. "So am I."

Her smile was wide, gentle. "Sometimes I still can't believe this is real…that you're really here."

Never looking away from the warmth in her eyes, he lifted a hand to cover hers. "Believe it," he said. "There's nowhere I'd rather be."

They sat quietly after that, watching Charlotte, hands joined, until the first rays of the August sun filled the nursery, and shadows gave way to the buttery warmth of a new day.

* * * * *

HARLEQUIN® *Super Romance*®

COMING NEXT MONTH

Available October 12, 2010

LARGER-PRINT BOOKS!

GET 2 FREE LARGER-PRINT NOVELS PLUS
2 FREE GIFTS!

HARLEQUIN *Super Romance*

Exciting, emotional, unexpected!

YES! Please send me 2 FREE LARGER-PRINT Harlequin® Superromance® novels and my 2 FREE gifts (gifts are worth about $10). After receiving them, if I don't wish to receive any more books, I can return the shipping statement marked "cancel." If I don't cancel, I will receive 6 brand-new novels every month and be billed just $5.44 per book in the U.S. or $5.99 per book in Canada. That's a saving of at least 13% off the cover price! It's quite a bargain! Shipping and handling is just 50¢ per book.* I understand that accepting the 2 free books and gifts places me under no obligation to buy anything. I can always return a shipment and cancel at any time. Even if I never buy another book from Harlequin, the two free books and gifts are mine to keep forever.

139/339 HDN E5PS

Name	(PLEASE PRINT)	
Address		Apt. #
City	State/Prov.	Zip/Postal Code

Signature (if under 18, a parent or guardian must sign)

Mail to the **Harlequin Reader Service:**
IN U.S.A.: P.O. Box 1867, Buffalo, NY 14240-1867
IN CANADA: P.O. Box 609, Fort Erie, Ontario L2A 5X3

Not valid for current subscribers to Harlequin Superromance Larger-Print books.

**Are you a current subscriber to Harlequin Superromance books
and want to receive the larger-print edition?
Call 1-800-873-8635 today!**

* Terms and prices subject to change without notice. Prices do not include applicable taxes. N.Y. residents add applicable sales tax. Canadian residents will be charged applicable provincial taxes and GST. Offer not valid in Quebec. This offer is limited to one order per household. All orders subject to approval. Credit or debit balances in a customer's account(s) may be offset by any other outstanding balance owed by or to the customer. Please allow 4 to 6 weeks for delivery. Offer available while quantities last.

Your Privacy: Harlequin Books is committed to protecting your privacy. Our Privacy Policy is available online at www.eHarlequin.com or upon request from the Reader Service. From time to time we make our lists of customers available to reputable third parties who may have a product or service of interest to you. If you would prefer we not share your name and address, please check here. ☐

Help us get it right—We strive for accurate, respectful and relevant communications. To clarify or modify your communication preferences, visit us at www.ReaderService.com/consumerschoice.

HSRLP10R

*See below for a sneak peek at
our inspirational line, Love Inspired®.
Introducing HIS HOLIDAY BRIDE
by bestselling author Jillian Hart*

Autumn Granger gave her horse rein to slide toward the town's new sheriff.

"Hey, there." The man in a brand-new Stetson, black T-shirt, jeans and riding boots held up a hand in greeting. He stepped away from his four-wheel drive with "Sheriff" in black on the doors and waded through the grasses. "I'm new around here."

"I'm Autumn Granger."

"Nice to meet you, Miss Granger. I'm Ford Sherman, from Chicago." He knuckled back his hat, revealing the most handsome face she'd ever seen. Big blue eyes contrasted with his sun-tanned complexion.

"I'm guessing you haven't seen much open land. Out here, you've got to keep an eye on cows or they're going to tear your vehicle apart."

"What?" He whipped around. Sure enough, mammoth black-and-white creatures had started to gnaw on his four-wheel drive. They clustered like a mob, mouths and tongues and teeth bent on destruction. One cow tried to pry the wiper off the windshield, another chewed on the side mirror. Several leaned through the open window, licking the seats.

"Move along, little dogie." He didn't know the first thing about cattle.

The entire herd swiveled their heads to study him curiously. Not a single hoof shifted. The animals soon returned to chewing, licking, digging through his possessions.

Autumn laughed, a warm and wonderful sound. "Thanks,

I needed that." She then pulled a bag from behind her saddle and waved it at the cows. "Look what I have, guys. Cookies."

Cows swung in her direction, and dozens of liquid brown eyes brightened with cookie hopes. As she circled the car, the cattle bounded after her. The earth shook with the force of their powerful hooves.

"Next time, you're on your own, city boy." She tipped her hat. The cowgirl stayed on his mind, the sweetest thing he had ever seen.

*Will Ford be able to stick it out in the country
to find out more about Autumn?
Find out in HIS HOLIDAY BRIDE
by bestselling author Jillian Hart,
available in October 2010
only from Love Inspired®.*

Copyright © 2010 by Jill Strickler

SHLIEXP1010

FROM #1 *NEW YORK TIMES*
AND *USA TODAY* BESTSELLING AUTHOR

DEBBIE MACOMBER

Mrs. Miracle on 34th Street...

This Christmas, Emily Merkle (just call her Mrs. Miracle) is working in the toy department at Finley's, the last family-owned department store in Manhattan.

Her boss (who happens to be the owner's son) has placed an order for a large number of high-priced robots, which he hopes will give the business a much-needed boost. In fact, Jake Finley's counting on it.

Holly Larson is counting on that robot, too. She's been looking after her eight-year-old nephew, Gabe, ever since her widowed brother was deployed overseas. Holly plans to buy Gabe a robot—which she can't afford—because she's determined to make Christmas special.

But this Christmas will be different—thanks to Mrs. Miracle. Next to bringing children joy, her favorite activity is giving romance a nudge. Fortunately, Jake and Holly are receptive to her "hints." And thanks to Mrs. Miracle, Christmas takes on new meaning for Jake. For all of them!

Call Me Mrs. Miracle

Available wherever books are sold
September 28!

MIRA®

www.MIRABooks.com

MDM2819

HARLEQUIN
Super Romance

Watch out
for a whole new look for
Harlequin Superromance,
coming soon!

The same great stories you love
with a brand-new look!

Unexpected, exciting
and emotional stories
about life and falling in love.

Coming soon!

HSRREVIT